HUNGRY HEART

VIOLET HAZE

Stoked Publishing House

*To love and all the ways it connects with those who
enrich our lives and expand our horizons.*

CHAPTER ONE

There's something wrong with me.

Not maybe.

Definitely.

There's no other explanation for what I'm thinking right now. What I'm feeling.

What exactly is the feeling bothering me so much?

The fact I'm extremely turned on by the strange man staring at me from across the cafe. I caught him out of the corner of my eye. I refuse to look at him and give him the satisfaction of knowing how he's affecting me. I've an inkling he knows precisely what his intense stare is doing to me; he probably does it to lots of women.

He just has that look about him. You know, the one where his ruffled wavy black hair that touches the nape of his neck just so is perfect, his face is slight scruffy but not enough to count as anything less than sexy, and his lowered eyes make you think he's not been out of bed long. Yes, he looks like he wants to go back to bed and take someone with him.

And I think the person he wants right now is me.

But, that's too bad, because I don't know him.

I'm also not single.

Not that me having a boyfriend is a deterrent. My boyfriend and I have a special arrangement. However, it doesn't mean I can do whatever I want, or fuck whomever I want.

There are rules.

And this man is making me want to break every single one of them.

Hence, why there's something really fucking wrong with me in this instant.

When my friend, Ethan, takes a seat across from me and blocks the view of the other man, I'm beyond grateful. I grin, which Ethan mirrors back at me, and nods at the latte he's placed in front of me.

"Drink up and tell me, what's up with Professor Ryan? He seemed to have a bug up his ass about something this morning," he says. "I wanted to bitch slap him."

Snickering at his scrunched up nose, which

makes him look silly but amuses me like nothing else, I take a sip of my latte and shrug. "I think he was pissed so many people were behind on their projects. He wanted to see what people had done, but nobody really did anything yet."

"Except you. You're always prepared. A teacher's pet."

"You don't get a perfect GPA by being lazy and leaving things until the last second," I tease him, knowing he's got a nearly perfect GPA even though he's a procrastinator. "Well, except you. You're almost there."

"We both know that teacher gave me an A-minus because she heard me bragging about how I never do my work 'til the last second and had a perfect GPA because I'm a genius." He gives me a mock scowl, then winks at me.

"You probably went too far with the genius comment."

He laughs and sits back in his chair, putting his hands behind his head as he turns to stare out the window. I swear, Ethan has the most flawless profile. He might be one of the few people I've ever met who has a near symmetrical face in all aspects like myself. We've been friends since we were babies. Our mothers had us in the same hospital on the same day and shared a room, and we've been pretty much inseparable every single day since. People often mistake us as relatives, since we share light brown hair and blue eyes, which is perfectly okay with both of us since we are completely platonic.

For the record, my life isn't like a romance novel. Ethan and I suddenly aren't going to say, "oh my god, I'm in love with you!" because no, it's just not like that. We are literally like brother and sister — I'm the sister he never had and he's the brother I never had. He has two older brothers, but me, I'm an only child and my parents pride and joy. And Ethan looks out for me in a way nobody else ever has and our relationship is sacred. Not even my boyfriend would dare to speak against how close we are if he were inclined to say something, which he isn't.

Ethan and I are solid. My boyfriend and I are solid.

And when Ethan leans over toward the window to squint at something, I find my eyes locked on the strange man across the cafe who looks up at that exact moment. He smiles at me, and I swear, I'm blown away.

Shit, shit, shit.

I'm in trouble.

Especially since I'm about to blatantly invite the trouble into my life.

"You know what," I say suddenly, standing up. "I want a chocolate chip muffin. I'll be right back."

Ethan nods, not really hearing me, focused on whatever it is he's gazing at out the window and I head to the counter to order. There is one person in front of me so I have to wait, and because people are predictable, it's only a moment or two before I feel the man stand behind me. I don't even have to look to know.

"I'm Benedict," he murmurs, leaning in close to my ear so his breath brushes me in an intimate manner. His deep voice is sexy just as I imagined it would be from simply looking at him.

I ignore the way it makes me feel and am direct as possible so he knows everything he needs to. "I'm taken."

"Are you?" He chuckles, still close to me even though he isn't touching me in any way. "So am I. Now, what's your name?"

Interesting. Well, he gets points for being honest, and I've no idea what his situation is, so I give him an honest answer. "I'm Caroline."

"Is that your boyfriend sitting with you?"

"No."

"A friend? A relative? Someone I have to worry about beating me up for speaking with you?"

I can't help it. I laugh at the question and turn to face him as the person in front of me continues to waffle about what they want to order. Our bodies are inches apart as he straightens, and I have to look up into his face because he's got a good six inches on my five-foot-five frame. And the first thing I notice is he's even more attractive up close. His face might have a five o'clock shadow, but it's blemish free, and his hazel eyes shine bright as he gazes down at me, his multi-colored tie emphasizing the various flicks of color in them.

"He's my friend," I say with a smile. "Since we were kids. He's like a brother, and no, he won't beat you up."

Benedict's eyes are even more vibrant, if that's even possible, as he lifts a hand to my hair and pushes it behind my ear. It's forward, has my stomach dropping and my heart careening, but I can't seem to find the heart to object to this simplest of touches. He seems as fascinated by me as I am by him and I need to see what he wants.

"How old are you, Caroline?"

"I'll be twenty-one tomorrow. You?"

"Nice." He drops his hand, stepping back as the cashier behind us announces the total to the person ordering, and smiles at me. "I'm thirty. But it doesn't matter. I just wanted to make sure you were legal."

Legal for what?

"May I help you?" The cashier asks from

behind me, and I turn around without saying anything in response to his comment, stepping up to the counter.

"Yes, I'd like a chocolate chip muffin please." I wait until she holds her hand out for the money, then give it to her and step aside with a glance back at Benedict. "Your turn."

"Oh," he replies with a naughty grin, removing himself from the line to stand next to me. "I don't want anything to eat. At least, not from this cafe."

I ignore the butterflies in my stomach at his suggestive words and roll my eyes at him instead. "I'm sure your girlfriend would love to know you're hitting on a girl that isn't her in this cafe."

He leans in at the same moment I feel his hand slide into my pocket, tugging me until my side is against his, and whispers in my ear, "We have an open relationship."

He says that as if he knows I'll know what it means as my eyes collide with his. Which I do, but he can't know that having just met me. Then, he steps back while removing his hand from my pocket and sliding it into his own. "My card is in your pocket, Caroline. Call me."

I don't get a chance to reply as he turns around and walks away, out the door in the blink of an eye. The other person working holds out my muffin and I take it from her, then head back to my seat where Ethan is waiting for me with a smirk on his face.

"Who was the guy all up in your space?"

"His name is Benedict." I take a bite of my muffin, scowling as his grin grows wide, and I lift a brow as if to say, 'what?'

"Ah, nothing. It's obvious he wants to fuck you."

A piece of muffin gets caught in my throat and I start coughing like mad. Ethan jumps up and pounds on my back, chuckling as I take a deep breath and lean forward to take a drink of my latte.

"Asshole," I say once I can breathe again.

"You say the same to me all the time about the girls who hit on me, Caro." He shrugs. "I wonder what Nathan will think."

Nathan is my boyfriend, and Ethan knows all about our arrangement. He doesn't necessarily approve, but the great thing is he loves me and trusts me enough to know I'm the only one who gets any say about how I live my life — in general and in the romance department.

"Nathan has someone else, as you know. I'm the one between us who hasn't had any interest in anyone besides him." I reach into my pocket and pull out the card, which is bare except for his name and number, and hold it up. "Benedict put this in my pocket and told me to call him. Said he's in an open relationship. The fact I have a boyfriend didn't seem to stop him from assuming I'd be interested."

"Because you are and he knew it." When my mouth drops open, Ethan rolls his eyes. "Come on now. You were seconds away from jumping into his arms. Your interest in him was written all over your face."

It's dumb to deny the obvious, although jumping into his arms is a bit of an exaggeration. "Well, he's gorgeous. Can you blame me?"

"Nope. Go for it." Ethan stands up and swipes his backpack from the chair beside him, tossing it over his shoulder as he winks at me. "We still meeting at the club?"

"Uh huh. Wouldn't miss having my first legal drink at the stroke of midnight for nothing."

He comes around the table and kisses my cheek. "Invite the soon-to-be boy toy." At my scoff, he laughs. "See ya there at eleven-thirty, Caro."

I finish eating my muffin and drinking my latte, then ten minutes later, I head home to prepare for my evening out.

CHAPTER TWO

Nathan and Rissa, his other girlfriend, are having sex when I arrive home.

I know this because I can hear her moans all the way at the front door, which I slam in a deliberate fashion to make them aware of my presence. Perfect, since this results in a sudden drop in her verbal announcements of pleasure.

Up until a year ago, I lived with Ethan. But once Nathan bought a house of his own, he insisted living together was the best for both of us. He made it clear staying close and connected with me was the most important thing to him, and I loved that he didn't want to live apart.

The rules of our relationship made it so the rules must be made clear to anyone we have interest in. This house is Nathan's and I'm the only other person who lives here. People we're with may sleep over, hang out, spend a day with us, but they can't live here. They aren't allowed to leave things here 'just in case' and that's the way we want it.

Other rules include always introducing the other people in our lives to each other first before we sleep with them, always use protection, and spending two nights with each other a week alone is mandatory. Respect is key as well, and nobody's allowed to disrespect either of us, or our relationship. If they do, it is to end immediately.

Of course, as I told Ethan, Nathan is the only one between us to have someone else, but even his relationship with Rissa developed slowly. It wasn't so much that she wasn't cool with it, but it's always a little awkward making it clear to someone they are welcome to hit on your boyfriend, and yes, even sleep with him as long as she doesn't try to come between us.

Nathan had been into Rissa the moment he met her, and pursuing her had been half the fun. I had even helped him. She thought we were joking when we sat her down and told her it was totally okay for her to like him. We told her our belief is that monogamy isn't necessary for a successful relationship; trust and honesty are. It's natural to want to sleep with others, and sleeping with or even dating additional people doesn't lessen your love for your other partner or partners.

I wasn't sure she really understood the concept of polyamory — that's many (poly) and love (amory), or more than one love in plain speak — thanks to the way society leads people to believe romantic love is only between two people and it's not possible for any other way to exist. But, she took us at our word that it was cool, and I'd even chuckled when she apologized and said she wasn't into girls, asking if threesomes were part of the rules to date him.

Her relief when I told her I was only into men had both Nathan and I cracking up.

After that, they'd began dating, and although it took a few weeks for her to relax around me, all was well now for the last six months.

And finally, it's my turn, because I've found someone who is into me.

That is, if he's telling the truth about being in an open relationship. Unfortunately, I'm all too aware of how many men will lie to sleep with you, and people in a true open relationship are more than happy to assure you it is true. Those who aren't willing to introduce you to their significant other to make sure are flat out lying.

But first, I need to talk to Nathan about Benedict and make sure inviting him out this evening is a good idea.

Putting my stuff in my room and walking

toward the kitchen to get a drink, I take out my phone and the card Benedict gave me. Setting him up as a contact first, I open up a message after taking a glass down from the cupboard and decide it will amuse me to see how long it takes for him to realize who is texting him.

"*Hey.*"

Opening up the fridge, I pour myself a glass of water from the Brita pitcher before putting it back in the fridge. My phone buzzes as I'm taking a drink and carrying them both to the living room, I sit down before opening it to see what he said.

"Hay is for horses."

"You sound like my mother," I reply with a grin, lifting my legs and crossing them, using the table as a foot rest. "She always says that."

"I bet she's hoping you'll quit saying it and say hello instead."

"Hello," is my smartass reply. "Is this Benedict?"

"Depends on who's asking."

"Hmm. I don't know..."

"Not a lot of people have my personal mobile, so you're either the really beautiful girl from the cafe, or an older lady I helped cross the street earlier today."

"Which would you prefer I be?"

"The older lady for sure. She's definitely more my type."

I laugh out loud, his teasing reply making it clear he knows it's me, as the bedroom door opens. I lift my head to look at the same time Nathan catches sight of me and smiles, pulling Rissa close and kissing her on the cheek before heading toward me.

"Bye Rissa," I say with a lift of my hand, leaning forward to put my phone on the table after removing my feet from their perch.

She blushes, gives me a little wave in return, and goes out the way I came in a mere ten minutes ago.

Nathan plops down on the couch next to me, putting his arm around my shoulders before pulling me in for a kiss with his minty fresh breath. He doesn't linger, pulling back to say, "Babe, how was your day?"

"Oh, you know, amazing as always." I lift my arms and put them around his neck with an impish grin. "Nothing like a riveting three-hour class on a bright, Saturday morning."

My phone buzzes on the table and I ignore it as Nathan wraps his arms around my waist and nuzzles my neck, dropping small kisses from my jaw and on down. "Better you than me."

"Mmm, I'm never doing it again."

"You said that last semester," he replies with a chuckle, pulling away from me with a final kiss as my phone buzzes again. "You gonna get that?"

"Sorry." Leaning forward, I pick up the phone and read the texts.

The first says, "I know it's you Caroline. I'm glad you decided to contact me, although I did say call me..." followed by, "When am I taking you out?"

"Who is it?"

I put the phone down without replying, giving Nathan my full attention, placing my hands over his as I lock our gazes. "I met someone earlier. I may go out with him."

"Yeah?" He pushes a hand through his hair, which is dark brown and cropped short, his equally dark brown eyes twinkling at me as his smile grows wider. "Where'd you meet him? What's his name?"

It's moments like these when I really appreciate and adore him and our relationship. I love that he's curious and interested and is happy for me, just like I was when he met Rissa.

"Benedict. And it was at the cafe where I was hanging with Ethan after class."

"You inviting him out tonight?"

"As long as you're good with it, yep."

"Then answer the poor guy back," he says,

groaning as the phone buzzes again. "I'm gonna go hop in the shower, and then go run a few errands."

"All right." I give him a kiss before he stands up, then slap his ass through his shorts as he walks past me. "Love you."

"Love ya too."

Taking the phone in hand as Nathan leaves the room, I text Benedict back. "We're going out tonight for my birthday so I can have a drink at midnight. You in?"

His reply is almost instantaneous: "Sure am. Where are we meeting?"

"It may also include me trying to dance and embarrassing myself. Club Play. You know it?"

"Yeah. My girlfriend and I are there all the time. We'll be there about 11."

"K. See you about 11:30."

"Can't wait."

I'm unable to keep the grin off my face as I stand up and walk toward the bathroom to surprise Nathan in the shower. This evening is going to be great and I can't wait.

CHAPTER THREE

Being a Saturday night, the club is packed when Nathan and I arrive. He has his arm around my waist, and I have a hand in his back pocket, both of us flashing the bouncer our IDs. Letting us pass with a nod, we step inside and are immediately consumed in the mob of people. Nathan pulls me close, forcing his way through the people until we reach the bar, where I take a seat on the empty stool while he stands behind me with his arms wrapped around my middle.

"He didn't stamp your hand," Nathan points out with a grin, and my eyes go wide as I realize he's correct, and answers me before I can ask the obvious question. "I stopped by earlier today while I was out and told him it was your birthday at midnight. He said just don't order before midnight. It's not illegal to not stamp your hand."

"That's awful trustworthy of him," I tease, and Nathan chuckles in my ear as he hugs me from behind.

"We've been coming here for two years now, babe. He knows us and trusts we won't break the rules." The bartender steps overs to us and raises an expectant brow. "I'll have whatever's on tap, and she'll have a coke until she turns twenty-one at midnight."

The guy looks down at my hand, then back up at us with a nod, and walks away to get our order as I say, "He's so going to make me show him my ID, you know that right?"

"Yep. But hey, we're following the law."

Right then, my phone buzzes, and I open it to find a message from Benedict. "Where are you? Are you here yet?"

"*Yeah,*" I text back as Nathan releases his hold on my waist with a smile, leaning back against the counter next to me, eye on the crowd. "At the bar getting a soda and waiting on Ethan to show up. You?"

"Be there in a sec."

I laugh and put my phone down as I touch my hand to Nathan's, getting his attention. "He says he's on his way over."

"Cool." The bartender sets down our drinks,

Nathan handing him a card as he says, "Go ahead and open a tab."

"Their drinks are on me this evening." Benedict's voice comes from out of nowhere, and I whirl on the stool to find him standing right behind me. He's so close to me my knees almost touch his legs. "Don't worry about it, Frank. Make sure you add yourself a nice tip at the end of the night, too."

I don't see what happens behind me, but in a second, Nathan stands up straighter, and steps closer to my side, placing his hand around my waist once more. And Benedict doesn't even blink at this, which is a point in his favor, holding out his right hand to Nathan with a smile.

"I'm Benedict, and you must be Caroline's boyfriend."

"Yeah." Nathan takes his hand to shake, and I look up into his face to see he's totally relaxed and smiling as well. "I'm Nathan. And you didn't have to get the drinks..."

Benedict releases Nathan's hand and waves a dismissive hand as his eyes find mine. "I own this place. And it's my pleasure."

Oh, I bet it is. And seriously, the owner of *Club Play*? I caught the eye of the owner of the place my boyfriend and I frequented all the time? I can't believe it, but next to me, Nathan whistles low, then laughs.

"Good luck with this one, babe. I'm gonna go find Rissa." He leans in and pecks my lips, then nods at Benedict. "Have fun you two."

Nathan grabs his beer and walks away, leaving me alone with Benedict, who stands where Nathan just vacated and stares down at me. "I'm glad you decided to come."

Something — perhaps it's the naughty glint in his eyes — tells me those words were absolutely meant as a promise for what he wanted to make me do, and therefore, his statement is a double entendre.

"Where's your girlfriend?" I raise a brow as he smiles and leans on the bar with one elbow as he quirks a brow. "You knew I'd want confirmation of your claim to openness."

He holds up a hand with three fingers without a word, then lowers them one by one in an exaggerated and slow fashion. When the final finger joins his fist, I don't even get to blink as a body crashes into Benedict.

"Honey, there you are! You said by the bar, but did you have to lean on it so I couldn't see you through the crowd? Geeze." The woman with long and curly red hair throws her arms around his shoulders and kisses him on the cheek in a flamboyant fashion, then turns to me and grins. "You must be Caroline. Nice to meet you."

It happens so fast I'm left with my mouth gaping open and Benedict laughs.

"Caroline, meet my girlfriend, Miranda." He leans down and kisses his girlfriends lips, then looks at me as he states, "Here's your proof you wanted to make sure she's real and all that jazz. Satisfied?"

"Oh yes," Miranda squeals, leaning forward and hugging me, and honestly, it's a tad awkward. She pulls back, and steps away from both of us. "You two have fun! I'm going back to Len. Later!"

She runs off before I can even speak, and Benedict holds out his hand. "Come with me."

"She—you—I—" I look to where she went to, then down at his hand, and back up at his face. "What?"

"Frank," Benedict calls out, and within seconds, the bartender asks 'yes?' as he stands by us, and Benedict tilts his head toward me. "Tell Caroline here who my girlfriend is and what she looks like."

"Uh, okay." He looks at me and I can tell he's confused by the request as he shrugs. "Tall. Name is Miranda. Curly red hair. Hyper in a way that sort of has me imagining how a chipmunk on crack would act—"

I bust out laughing, cutting him off with a wave of my hand, and stand up. "Okay, okay, I believe you. But I'm still waiting for Ethan to show up. He's late."

"Text him and tell him to text you when he arrives. We'll come back and join in when he arrives. I'd like to go to my office where it's quiet and talk."

"Okay." I do as he says, then slide the phone into my tiny purse and pick up my soda. "Ready when you are."

He leads the way and as we enter the office, he shuts the door and therefore, shuts out all the sounds from the club, leaving us all alone.

CHAPTER FOUR

His office is warm and inviting.

Everything in the office is in black or silver, and therefore so sleek looking I'm afraid to touch anything, but he doesn't seem to have that problem.

Benedict walks over to the bar in the wall and pours himself a drink, then turns and motions for me to sit on the leather couch against the wall near him. I walk over and take a seat, sitting my purse down on the floor in front of the couch. A moment or two later, he's sitting next to me; real close to me, with our legs touching. He rests his left hand right above my knee, and the other holds his drink as we sit there in companionable silence.

It doesn't last long as he asks, "How long have you and Nathan been together?"

I'm glad he's asked this question. Knowing all

the details about each other is a good start, and I'll be honest, I'm not sure what I expected this evening. However, it wasn't that we'd be sitting in his office inside *Club Play* having a chat.

Not that I'm complaining. And even though he seems well-put together, and definitely wants me, he seems rather unsure, which is absolutely endearing.

"Three years, almost four now. We started dating when I was seventeen and he was twenty. What about you and Miranda?"

He clear his throat, his lips curving as he turns his body toward mine a little, and catches my gaze. "Eight years. We met as freshmen in college, but didn't begin dating until after we graduated."

"She seems..." I pause, looking for the right word, but finish with a lame, "nice."

"Oh, she is bat-shit crazy, but she always has been."

The statement is full of affection, but I'm not sure what to say in reply, so I take a sip of my soda, and let my curiosity take over as I examine the room. He doesn't say anything more and when my eyes finally return to him, it's to discover him staring at me with hungry eyes.

"I've never done this before," he admits, setting his glass on the side table before turning toward me even more. "I'm not sure of the rules..."

Not what I expected him to say.

"Wow." I copy his motions and set my glass on the table beside me, then place my hands in my lap. "Um...so whose idea was it to open up the relationship?"

"Hers. It took her a year to convince me."

"And you guys didn't set up any rules?"

"Oh." He nods. "Yes, we did. Did you?"

"Yeah." I elaborate when he lifts a brow, indicating his curiosity. "Use protection, introduce first, no disrespect or the person is gone, and a mandatory two nights together a week. Keeps the drama to a minimum and expectations clear."

"And is there a timeline...?"

I assume he means to go from meeting to dating and being together while with another.

"No." His gaze sharpens at my reply, his hands going to my lap with one on each bare knee, and I ask him the questions I need to know the answers to. "What do you want, Benedict? What are your expectations of this? And why approach me?"

"I cheated a little. I've seen you and your boyfriend here, many times, but I've also seen him with Rissa. So I asked about you. I knew all about your relationship before I approached you." I suck in a breath of air as his hands slide up my legs and tease the edge of my miniskirt. "I knew you'd know where I'm coming from and getting involved with a person whose single seems a bit too risky to me. Plus, I find you extremely attractive."

His explanation made his approach in the cafe make complete sense, even though his questions had obviously been nonsense since he knew who my boyfriend was and my age. I can only appreciate his confidence in declaring his interest in me in such a bold way. But..."I'm not interested in *just* having sex with someone else. So if that's your interest...?"

"No." He rises a little and leans over me, until I'm lying on my back and he's above me, in between my legs with his hands coming to rest on each side of my head. "I'm not either. I'm not that type of man."

Our lips are so close, and I admit it, I'm extremely turned on by our position. He smells amazing, he's gorgeous, and he wants me. And I wish he'd lean in and kiss me, but I feel the hesitation to go forward in him, and ask him one final thing.

"Does she already have someone else? That Len person she mentioned...?"

"Yes. For a year now. They adore each other." His eyes drop to my lips as I lick them, then back up to my eyes where the fire in them has relit. "I could've been seeing others this whole time, but I waited. I didn't want just anyone. I wanted someone who could potentially mean the same thing to me as she does, because it's only due to how much I love her that I was able to realize she needed more than I can give her. And also, how much I needed more than she could give me as well."

I don't say anything in reply. There's nothing I can say in response to that. It was sweet, and honest, and sincere, reminding me of something Nathan would say to anyone who questioned him about his feelings for me.

Instead, I place my hands on his shoulders, lifting my head off the couch until our lips press against one another as I make a decision for both of us. And it's such a sweet, gentle, closed-mouth kiss; the kind where you both want it, and you're not sure how far you can go, or how fast. His lips are soft yet firm, the taste of the scotch he drank on them, and with our mouths simply pressed together, I'm the first to give in. I open mine a little and he groans, his weight coming down on me more, pressing me into the sofa as his tongue invades my mouth with no sign of his earlier hesitation in sight.

He moves and readjusts as we continue kissing, and then his hand is on my thigh and moving up under my skirt. Already riding up due to our position, it's not long until he's cupping my ass in his hands and making appreciative sounds into my mouth as he gives the cheek a squeeze.

Sliding my hands up in his hair, I grab some as I rock my body up into his, which has him rocking into me in return. Our mouths alternate between tongues tangling and simple kissing, and his hand doesn't move from my ass. We just lie here, kissing, and it's the first time in a long while I've done nothing else but kiss.

I admit, after three years with Nathan, and only kissing and having sex with Nathan, this feels weird to me. But not bad weird; just unique in that it will be my first time right along with Benedict. Nathan was my first everything, and it looks like Benedict will be my second everything. But first...

"Benedict," I whisper as I pull my lips away and meet his questioning gaze. "I feel like if we're going to be kissing, your hand is going to be on my ass, and we're going to be together...I should know your last name since I assume you already know mine." My lips curve up into a smile as he laughs.

"Yes, I do." He gives me a soft kiss on the lips and says, "Benedict Grant, at your service, Miss Caroline Lowther."

"Nice to meet you, Mister Grant," I tease him back, which makes him squeeze my ass in response, and lower his mouth back to mine.

And then, my phone buzzes a few seconds later, making Benedict pull away and sit up.

He grins as he looks down at his watch while I return to my previous sitting position. "You should get that. It's two minutes until midnight and almost time for your first legal drink!"

I reach down for my purse and pull out my phone to see a text message from Ethan.

"Birthday girl, birthday boy needs you. I heard the hot guy you met is the owner of this club and I know you're probably kissing him right now, but get out here to the bar!"

I laugh and read the text off to Benedict, who then takes my hand with a grin and says, "Let's go."

And as we walk out the door and toward my friends, he doesn't let go of my hand, which is as close to a declaration as you can get without saying a word that we're together.

An hour later, Nathan is sitting in a booth with Rissa, I'm sitting on a stool at the bar with Benedict next to me at another, Miranda is dancing up close and personal with Len, and then there is Ethan.

Standing on the other side of me, Ethan's back is against the bar and his arms crossed, and he's majorly drunk.

I stopped at two drinks, as I've never been interested in getting drunk, but Ethan has no qualms about such things. And now, he's been going on and on about being single for the last ten minutes, which Benedict apparently finds amusing because he has to keep hiding his smile.

While I adore Ethan, he's single because he's not so great at approaching females, and even though I tried to practice with him, it had just made us laugh silly because it's hard to flirt with someone you consider your sibling. And I'm not sure how to help him, which makes the moment Benedict jumps in to save me from Ethan's drunk ramblings all the more special.

"Ethan, I think I know someone you might like," Benedict says as he stands, leaning over to kiss my cheek before straightening. "Follow me."

He walks over before Ethan has a chance to digest what he said, and gives me a startled look. I shrug and nod my head in the direction he went, indicating Ethan should just follow him. Which he does, and I'm left all alone.

I turn back to the bar and order a soda from Frank, who is now one of two bartenders instead of being all alone, and he leans over to speak with me as he hands me my drink.

"Having fun?"

"Yeah! I love this place. It's always so busy and crowded, but it has great energy."

"I like how I'm not deafened by the music all night, six nights a week."

"Right? People can still have fun without the music being turned up to an ear-drum busting level."

He grins at me, nodding, as another customer approaches but the other bartender waves a hand to indicate she has it.

"Have you known Benedict long?" I ask, taking a sip of my soda, watching as his brow lifts. "I mean, how long have you worked here?"

"Since the day it opened almost six years ago. He's a great guy," he says, seeming to gather what I want to ask but don't.

I lean in, crooking my finger to indicate he should give me his ear, and when he does, I ask in a low voice, "And his girlfriend? Is she...okay?"

He pulls away a little and stares at me, but he must see the question is an honest one because he grimaces, and with a quick dart around us tells me, "She's not...right in the head. I think she's bad for him, but he loves her and wants to protect her. I don't believe she loves him, and she spends a lot of time with Len. He doesn't show how much it hurts him, but I've spent a lot of time around him since we met, and I can tell. I asked him why he allows it and he says it's because otherwise, she would've left him completely. He doesn't seem to agree with me when I said she sort of already has since she moved out six months ago into her own place, saying she needs some space."

Wow. I'm not sure I should know this, but glad I'm aware of the situation. And the worry is clear in his face and words, so I can't fault him for sharing since I asked.

"So, I've walked right into a mess is what you're saying?"

"It's like that?" At my nod, he grins. "Perhaps, but maybe dating you will make him see the light. Like I said, he's the good guy here."

He steps back, his eyes leaving mine, and a few seconds later, I realize why when arms encircle my waist and Benedict whispers in my ear, "Dance with me."

I let him drag me away and soon we're in a dark corner, our bodies flush together, with his hands on my hips. My arms are around his neck and we're slow dancing, but I can tell he wishes he could let his hands roam, and part of me wants to let them.

The other part of me wonders if I should walk away now with what Frank told me. But I can't even bring it up to Benedict because I wouldn't want to get Frank fired for sharing information he probably shouldn't have. Benedict is obviously pretending everything is fine, so I'm not sure what to do. I don't need to invite drama into my life, and certainly not into my relationship with Nathan, yet I like Benedict and he might need someone when it all finally blows up in his face. Which it sounds like it will, at least from what Frank has said.

Why I feel like that person should be me isn't something I can explain, but I decide I'm willing to risk it.

"Tell me what nights you spend with Nathan every week," he whispers into my ear before nipping at it, making me shiver and sigh, my serious thoughts drifting away as I answer him.

"Monday and Friday, always." I lick my lips, lifting my gaze to meet his just in time to see them light up. "Why?"

"Spend the night with me tonight. And by spend the night, I mean, cuddle for a little while and fall asleep next to me."

He moves his hands up to my waist as I ask, "That's it?"

His grin takes a decidedly naughty turn, and along with a gleam in his eye, I'm a sucker for it. A sucker for him and he knows it.

He backs me up until I'm against the wall, shadowed where nobody could see us unless they were really looking, and captures my lips in a long, sweet kiss before saying against them, "That's it until we wake up. After that, all bets are off. So, what do you say?"

I say yes because I like him and don't want to resist how I feel. After I let Nate know where I'm going, Benedict takes me home with him.

CHAPTER SIX

When I open my eyes the next morning, the first thing I notice is Benedict is snoring into my ear. It's soft, but because he's so close, it's undeniable, and I smother a giggle to avoid waking him.

Last night, Benedict kept to his word. After arriving at his place, we stripped down to our underwear, climbed under the comforter, and snuggled up to one another. Him as the big spoon, me as the little, and it didn't take long for me to pass out. In what I consider an amazing feat, we stayed in the same position the whole night.

Cute, until I wake up needing to go to the bathroom. Wiggling out of from under his arm, trying not to wake him the whole time, I'm successful and walk softly until I reach it. A few minutes later, I wash my hands, then put some of his toothpaste on my finger and rub my teeth and tongue. Probably could look and with no doubt find an extra toothbrush but I don't wanna take too long.

Tiptoeing back to the bed, I slip beneath the blankets and am almost under his arm when his sleepy eyes open.

"Hey." His voice is low and smooth as if he wasn't just sound asleep moments before.

"Hi."

My reply comes out as a squeak because with amazing speed he's wrapping me in his arms and pulling me close to body so we're touching in every place possible.

"I haven't slept like that in a while," he says before dipping his head and pressing a kiss on my naked shoulder. "I almost forgot how great a full night's rest could make me feel."

Between the sound of his voice, the fact his simple kiss has my whole left side tingling, and the way he's holding me skin-to-skin, I know what I feel and it's not anything I'll soon forget.

Straight and pure lust.

Having watched him undress last night, I'm sure my body is reacting to him in a primal way. Under his civilized clothing, he's divine. He's muscular, his body defined, and I don't believe he has an ounce of fat anywhere on him.

Except his ass. He's got a terrific ass and that's

from seeing him in his boxers. There's a chance seeing him completely nude will cause me to faint.

Giggling at my thoughts, he lifts his head and stares me in the eyes, his own glinting with what I'm sure are his own wicked musings.

"You know what I like about you, Caroline?"

I hear his words, but my eyes drop to his mouth the moment it moves, and all I can manage to say in response is, "Huh?"

His hand, the one free below the blankets to explore my body, begins to do exactly that. From where his palm rested on my hip, he drags the tip of fingers up my side and back down, then returns, pausing on the curve of my breast.

"I like how everything you feel and want is written all over your face."

"Is it? And what do I want?" I feel lame, but that's all I can come up with since I'm distracted by the touch of his hand.

"Me." Cupping my breast in his hand, he gives it a gentle squeeze, using his thumb to tease the nipple as he rubs it back and forth over it. "If I touched you right now, would your body be ready? Would you be slick and ready to receive my cock deep inside you with one, quick thrust?"

"Wow." My eyebrows raise even as I grin, pleased with his dirty talk. "Well, that escalated quickly."

"You didn't answer my question," he says, ignoring what I've said completely while his hands continue to roam.

"Mmm. Why don't you find out for yourself?" Covering his hand with mine, he lets me slide it down my body in-between the both of us. Before I can slip his hand between my legs, he stops me, my invitation clear.

"Hands above your head," he commands, releasing my hand and tossing the blanket aside, baring me to his eyes.

Raising one arm and then the other, I do as he says while he readjusts my position, takes off my underwear, then opens my legs to slide between them before I can even check him out.

"Ben—"

That's as far as I get before his lips are on my lips, his tongue seeking entrance. When I give him what he wants, his left hand glides down, lifts my leg around his waist, and after a second, he does exactly as he promised he would. In one quick thrust, he's deep inside me and my gasp is lost in his mouth, my fingers wrapping tight around the tiny posts in the headboard as my body adjusts to his size.

Since my only sexual experience is with Nathan, I can't help but compare. Even though I'm so turned on Benedict's entry didn't hurt, he is bigger. And the over-full feeling alone makes me tense up while the sensations have my whole body tingling with awareness.

Benedict stays still, making it clear he's paying attention to how I'm feeling, and breaks our kiss to growl against my lips, "Fuck, you're tight. Are you okay?"

"Yes." The word comes out as more of a squeak and I suck in a breath at realizing something. "Please tell me you put on a—"

He cuts me off with a brush of his mouth against mine, then says, "Yes. I woke up while you were in the bathroom and did it then. I wouldn't break your rules."

Nice. Guess that's when he took off his boxers as well. "Sneaky, but—"

Reaching up, he grabs one of my hands and brings my arm down, sliding between our bodies until I can feel where we're connected, and the undeniable proof. Then he lets go and I just grab ahold of the post above my head again when he pulls back out and then in once more, hard enough to take my breath away.

"Have you ever come from simply being fucked, Caroline?"

"N-no."

He chuckles, and if I had to guess, it's in response to my stuttering. "Do you want to?"

"I don't think I can."

"Well," he says, pausing to give me a long, sweet kiss, "can't know 'til you try." Flexing the hand he's using to hold onto my left side, he moves it to grip my ass. "I'm going to hold onto this side here while I fuck you hard and fast." With the other hand, he caresses my right thigh. "You'll move this one as you see fit until I'm hitting you just right on the inside. Your g-spot, specifically."

He stares at me, and it takes me a minute to realize he's waiting for me to say something.

"Okay."

"Relax," he says, withdrawing nice and slow when I do, then sinks back in with single, swift thrust.

"Oh god." It feels great, but I want to see if moving my leg will make it even better, so I spread my legs a little wider. "Do it again."

"I like a woman who gives direction almost as much as I enjoy giving it."

"Then why aren't you—"

He's out and plunging back in so hard and fast the words turn into a small scream, his eyes slamming shut as he grips my ass seconds before I close my own eyes at the burst of pleasure throughout my body.

"Grip the other side and lift just a little," I

whisper, refusing to open my eyes, and without saying a word, he does what I ask.

And when he moves again, it's clear I've found the perfect position as he does exactly as he promised, fucking me hard and fast. I can barely breathe, but I don't even notice as stroke after stroke of his cock keeps me in an ever-increasing spiral of delicious desire. The feeling spreads through my limbs, my body going taut as the orgasm overtakes me, ripping incoherent noises from my throat before I can stop them. Benedict gives one final thrust and joins me a second later with a loud groan of his own, and then covers me with his body.

He stays in place, and I assume he's resting on his elbows because he's not crushing me. I feel his lips cover mine as he gives me a soft, gentle kiss.

"Beautiful." He cups my face in his hand, using the pad of his thumb to caress my cheek, and chuckles as I move into his touch with a content sigh. "Caroline, look at me."

"Mm, mm. Not sure I can open my eyes even if I wanted to. Which I don't. 'Cuz wow."

He replaces the feel of his thumb with his lips, giving me small pecks on the cheek, down to my lips, and back again. Finally lowering my arms, I wrap them around his neck and when his mouth connects with mine again, I move to capture his bottom lip with the bite of my teeth. When I release it, he returns the action in kind with a growl, then says against my mouth, "Be right back."

"Mmkay." Dropping my arms to the bed with the realization he's going to clean up, my eyes remain closed as he climbs off me, leaving me and my nude lethargic body all alone.

And I don't remember him returning to me since I fall asleep.

CHAPTER SEVEN

Benedict's cooking in the kitchen when I wake up an hour later and go to find him.

"Tell you what," he says with a laugh as I enter and sit down at the table, my face flaming. "That's the first time I've ever put a woman to sleep by having sex with her. My life is complete."

"Shut up."

He doesn't, continuing to chuckle as he walks over with spatula in hand, and leans over to kiss me on the lips before stepping back with a smile. "Coffee? Orange juice? Vodka?"

"Vod—" I hold up a hand, confused. "What? Why would I want vodka with breakfast?"

He shrugs, walking back over to the stove and stirring something, chuckling once again. "Hey, I didn't know what you like to drink in the morning. So what'll it be?"

"Uh, orange juice, I guess." Finally noticing the delicious smell of breakfast, my stomach grumbles, and I cover it with my hands. "Whatcha making?"

"Eggs. Bacon. Sausage. Good for you?"

"Yummy." Standing up, I feel a stretch coming on and lift my arms, rising up on my tiptoes while letting out a yawn.

Before I can even return to my original position, Benedict is across the room, lifting me off the ground and sitting me on the tabletop.

"God, you're beautiful." With one hand on the back of my neck, his other hand lands on my thigh, moving up and up until it slides between my legs. When he finds nothing impeding his touch from going further, he groans, and pulls his hand away. "Shit. Why didn't you put your underwear on? And you're real fucking hot in my shirt. I'm gonna fuck you with it on."

"What you're gonna do is burn the eggs," is all I say even though his arousing words have me wanting him to make good on his statement.

With a curse, he steps away and whirls around, heading back to the stove as I hop down off the table.

"I'll get some juice — and something to wipe the table off with."

Neither of us say anything as I do as I've said and he finishes cooking the food. Then, when we're both at the table with our plates in front of us, the silence while we eat is companionable. And once again, I can't help but compare it to my life with Nathan.

Any time Nathan and I are together, he's usually speaking a mile a minute — about his work, about Rissa, about his grand plans for himself or for both of us, etcetera — and I'm the one listening with a smile on my face. Of course, Nathan would listen if I had a lot to say, but I don't in general. I've always been the more quiet one of both of us. And it's never been an issue, the fact we clicked that way perfect in our minds.

And now...well, now I'm having breakfast in peace and quiet, with the occasional hot glance from Benedict making me wish we were back in bed. My desire is reflected in his gaze and I know he wishes he were touching me instead of eating.

God, the sex had blown my mind. He'd joked he'd never put a woman to sleep, but in truth, I'd never fallen asleep after sex in the morning either. It's always energized me and got me going, but the sex with him and the orgasm...wow indeed. I've had regular orgasms — by my own hand or with Nathan — and yet, none of them have ever fucking felt like the one earlier had.

"If you keep giving me with that 'fuck me' look, you won't be finishing breakfast, Caroline."

His words jolt me out of my reverie, where I realize I'm staring at him quite rudely, and biting my lip to boot. With a blush, I take a drink of my juice, averting my eyes as I say, "You really like saying my name, don't you?"

"Yes, I do. It rolls off my tongue nicely." Putting down his fork and pushing his plate away and to the side, he holds out a hand to me. "C'mere."

When I focus on him once more and hesitate, he uses his other hand to pull my plate toward him, lifting a brow in question. Then, he pats his lap while pushing his chair a little bit away from the table so there's enough room for me to join him.

Placing my hand in the one he holds out, I stand up and walk the few steps to him. He pulls me down into his lap, making sure I'm facing away, and moves my hair to one side before pressing a kiss on my neck.

"Eat," he murmurs in my ear, giving the top of it a small nip with his teeth at the same time he spreads open my legs like he wants them. "Can't let the birthday girl starve."

He's not wearing anything but a pair of shorts, and I can feel his erection pressing against my ass. Ignoring it, I pick up a piece of bacon and take a bite, my action simultaneous with Benedict's hand sliding up my thigh, then cupping me between my legs.

When he slips one finger inside of me, followed by a second, the rest of my food is forgotten. Pushing it to the side, my head falls forward, and I grip the edge of the table as I move into his hand.

After another kiss on the nape of my neck, he slowly stretches me, inserting another finger before curling his hand and stroking the spot he'd fucked a response out of earlier. A whimper slips past my lips as the pleasure of his touch sends sparks of arousal to every inch of me.

"Listen to me, Caroline," he says with a small laugh, removing his hand before sliding them around to cup my ass. "Lift up and hold yourself that way for a minute."

Doing as he says, his hands leave me and I hear rustling, followed by the distinct sound of him opening up a condom packet. "God, you planned this?"

With a muffled laugh, one of his hands returns to my ass, caressing it before skimming his fingers down, then around my thigh, and finally back between my legs. Using two fingers to spread my arousal around and tease my clit a little, he presses his hand to me, saying, "Lower yourself onto me. I'll guide you."

As the tip of his cock finally nudges at my pussy, even my arousal can't prevent the slight sting

I feel at his entrance, and he pauses when a hiss slips out of my mouth.

"Do I need to stop?" A shake of my head is all he needs to bring me down further, until he's deep inside me, and I'm clutching the table for dear life. "You're even tighter in this position, Caroline. Holy fuck."

I clench the muscles around his cock in response, loving the way he purrs my name every time he says it. His hands, which have moved from between my legs to rest on my hips, grip them as he rocks his body up into mine.

"Oooh."

"You like that?" Bringing one arm around my lower body as I whisper 'yes,' he uses the other to grip my hair and wraps it around his hand, tilting my head toward him, along with making it so I must arch my back. "I have a...certain thing I enjoy. I'd like to share it with you."

My heart goes careening at those words, unsure if he's about to show me something I won't want to know about after all. "Oh...okay?"

"I'm going to rest your upper half on the table," he says while standing up in one swift motion after releasing my hair, putting me into position quick, until my cheek comes into gentle contact with the cool surface. "As for what I like...grab the edge of the table and hold on."

The table isn't huge, so with how I'm laying, it's easy to do as he commands. He straightens my legs, although he keeps them slightly spread, and pushes up the back of the shirt I'm wearing to bare my back. Running one hand down my spine, he clasps one hip with the other and lifts, so the lower half of me isn't touching the table at all.

"I'm going use you, Caroline." The hand sliding down my back leaves, only to come back down with a hard slap on my ass, and the way he's holding me means when I react instinctively, I'm unable to move. "I loved pleasuring you earlier, but now, you'll simply be what I take my pleasure from, and you aren't to take any from it, understand?"

I bite my lip to keep from telling him what he's saying pleasures me all on it's own. My nipples are rock hard, even pressed into the table as they are, and so as a compromise I simply go, "Mmhmm," because I can't trust opening my mouth right now. And I know it's all a game, one I'm willing to play along with.

"No moaning, no gasping; no sounds at all." He slaps my ass, testing my comprehension, and I hold back from giving any reaction at all, but just barely. "Those hands don't move, Caroline. You simply lie here with your beautiful, luscious body, and please me."

When he begins to move, I use all my energy

focusing on not making a noise. Biting my lip, holding back a moan when his cock strokes me just right, and making sure I don't move at all.

My conclusion is his certain thing he enjoys is something I enjoy and is as hot as fuck.

And I'm good at doing what he wants, getting a private thrill out of doing my hardest to make no noise, until he smacks my ass again, leaving me unable to prevent my body from being tipped over the edge of an orgasm so intense my body shakes.

"Tsk tsk, Caroline," he says, but I hear the smile in his voice as he gives a final thrust and comes with a groan of his own.

"Shush, Benedict. It's your fault."

He laughs at my mumbled words, bringing his body down on mine, and pressing a kiss on the crook of my neck.

"Time for a shower, birthday girl," he says.

And off we go.

CHAPTER EIGHT

It's six in the evening by the time I arrive home.

After our shower, we ended up cuddling on the couch, and Benedict let me choose the movie. So I chose a romantic comedy I hadn't seen before, and he enjoyed it more than I did.

One nap, some late lunch, and a walk in the park later, he dropped me off at home.

Taking off my shoes, I change into something more comfy, then head into the living room to find Nathan sitting on the sofa watching television, all alone. Without saying a word, I plop onto the couch beside him, automatically leaning in to him, and he wraps his arm around my shoulder.

"Happy birthday, baby." Giving my shoulder a squeeze, he kisses the top of my head. "How was your night?"

"Humph."

"That good huh?"

"Honestly," I say, laughing while snuggling closer. "I had a great time."

"Good."

We're both quiet after that.

I've never asked Nathan specifics regarding his and Rissa's time together. It's not necessary for either of us to go into details, even though we've all hung out many times. It's not weird to us, but we also don't flaunt our love life around because we understand people are uncomfortable with it. Doesn't mean they aren't aware of it; it's just the discussing of it that's unnecessary.

And on a personal level, I don't want to know what they do or when they do it, which is why I believe Nathan doesn't ask about my time with Benedict, and that's just perfect for me.

My phone buzzes in my pocket, so I pull it out and see a text from Ethan.

"So how was the sex?"

"Who says we had sex? And who did he introduce you to?"

"Ha! Please. You two were almost having sex on the dance floor. I was afraid you were going to set each other on fire. As for the girl, well..."

"We were not! We didn't have sex til this morning, so ha to you! And...?"

"Guess that makes us both sluts then becuz I totally got laid...I think I like your new boyfriend."

"You fucked Benedict? Ew!"

"Shut up. :D No. Her name is Destiny and now she's my girlfriend."

I laugh out loud at this, and Nathan turns to look at me. "What's funny?"

"Last night Benedict introduced Ethan to this girl and I guess her name is Destiny. And now they had sex and are dating."

"Cool," he says with a shrug before returning his focus to the show, allowing me to text Ethan back again.

"I'm happy for you. When do I get to meet her?"

"NEVER! ;)"

"Ha. Well, I'll see you in the morning, you can tell me everything then. I'm gonna go spend the rest of my birthday with Nathan."

"K. Love ya."

"Love ya too."

Slipping the phone back in my pocket, I switch my focus back to Nathan, gazing up into his face until his lips quirk and his eyes are on me.

"Why're you staring at me?"

"Because you're hot and I love you."

"Ditto. You look even more hot with your cheeks all flushed like they are." His face goes a bit serious as he lifts a hand to mine, using the back of it to stroke my cheek. "First time I've seen you look so pleased in a while."

I frown at this, shocked he thinks such a thing. "What? You please me all the time."

"Oh, I know." With a grin, he moves the remote to the table, then grabs me by the waist and lifts, until I'm straddling his lap while facing him. "But the way you looked at him last night as he approached us, I was jealous for a second."

My heart jumps at his words, biting my lip in a nervous manner, even though his whole demeanor makes it clear he's happy and amused. His eyes search mine as he slides his hand to the nape of my neck and pulls our faces close until our breaths mingle.

"You know you're my number one," I feel the need to say, lifting my hands to rest on his shoulders for a moment before I slide them across toward his neck, then up it until I'm cradling his face. "Nobody can ever take your place with me."

"Of course not. We're nothing alike, which is why I was only jealous for a second and nothing more." His eyes blaze, his free hand sliding up my soft pajama pant covered leg until he reaches my waistband, slipping it down and inside as my breath hitches. "But the flush... I remember that flush well. You looked at me the same way when we met, the desire to be close to me written all over your face."

With a giggle, I give him a soft peck on the lips before wrapping my arms around his neck, moving my lower body into his touch as he slips his hand between my legs. "I've never been able to hide how I feel, you know that. I want you even more now than when we met."

"It's obvious to me, but less to the world." He takes advantage of my lack of underwear, which I'd forgone during my change after returning home, gliding a finger through my arousal until he can and does penetrate me, making me gasp because of how sensitive I am. "How much you want me is evident in the way you watch me when you think I'm not looking; in how you always have to touch me in some way no matter what we're doing; when I'm engrossed in my work and you bring me everything I need without a word. You please me in every way. It's no wonder why you've got me wrapped around your little finger."

"Ummm. Pretty sure it's your finger with all the magic right now."

He laughs, but it mingles with my gasp as he thrusts another one inside me, and disappears completely as he seizes my mouth with his. We kiss each other with a sweetness mixed with a hunger and a familiarity only time spent together brings.

Our love is clear between us here, in these moments when all our focus is on each other and nothing else, our desire burning bright in our touch; something not even I can adequately articulate.

And moments later, when he stands up in one fluid motion, he carries me to our room, our lips never breaking contact until he places me upon the bed.

"I love you," he says then while stripping out of his clothing, mine following his pretty quickly.

Wrapping my legs around him as he gets between them, my lips curve in happiness as my arms encircle his neck and right before our lips meet, I respond, "I love you, too."

After that, there are no more words between us.

Just the love and passion of two people who believe they couldn't be more perfect for one another.

"Caro, are you paying attention?"

Jerked from my daydreaming by a poke in the arm from Ethan, I lift my head to glare at him. "What?"

"That's a no," he mutters even as he grins at me. "My girlfriend's coming this way."

He barely gets the words out before a girl passes me with a squeal, making me wince at the same time she throws her arms around Ethan's neck. All I see is dark red hair, freckled skinny arms with a helluva whole lot of bangles on her wrists, and the fact she's only slightly shorter than him because she's pulled him into a kiss. It's been a whole three days since they were introduced and according to Ethan, they've spent every minute together that they can. That means we spend less time together, but I will have to remember to thank

Benedict because from everything Ethan's said, they are perfect for one another.

My phone buzzes so I rip my eyes away from their overt display of affection and my internal thoughts to see who sent me a text.

Noticing it's from Benedict makes me happy as does reading what he asks. "Miss me?"

But I wouldn't be me if I didn't mess with him a little. "I'm sorry. Who is this again? ;)"

"Benedict. Who is this? ;)" His reply is instantaneous and I laugh at realizing he's returning my 'fucking with' favor.

"Sorry I don't know anybody by that name... perhaps you have the wrong number?"

"Perhaps you'd like to take a ride on my cock later? That might jog your memory."

My face burns as Ethan says, "Caroline, this is Destiny. Destiny, my best friend Caroline."

Looking up to discover she's sitting next to him now, I put my phone down on the table and smile. "Hi. I've heard a lot about you in the last three days."

Leaning forward with her hands clasp and elbows on the table, her cheerful grin gives me the impression she's a rather joyful person. I can see why Ethan likes her. "Have you? Same here 'cuz Ethan's told me so much about you! And y'all look so much alike."

"Yeah, we get that a lot."

When she sighs, it has a dreamy quality to it, and she hooks her arm around Ethan's while leaning into him. "Y'all are so lucky. I grew up all over the place, so didn't have the chance to spend time with one person."

My phone buzzes, but I ignore it in the spirit of being polite. "Why's that? Military brat?"

"Ha! No. My parents just liked traveling the world so they homeschooled me and took me along with 'em. It was kinda cool honestly."

"Neat." Glancing at Ethan to find him one hundred percent focused on her, I lean back in my chair and ask, "So how d'you know Benedict?"

"Who?" Her confusion only lasts a moment before she laughs and says, "Oh! Right. Gosh, he's friends with my brother, they met as freshmen in college. So I've known him forever, like, since I was nine."

When my phone goes off once more, she points at it and smiles wide. "You should probably get that. Somebody obviously wants to get ahold of you awful bad."

"Yeah." Picking it up, I give her a sheepish smile of my own. "Sorry. Just a sec."

"No big deal." She turns toward Ethan. "Let's get something to eat, I'm starving."

They take off without giving me another glance

and I read what Benedict's sent me: "I don't believe I've shocked you into silence. Are you okay? Do you need CPR? I'd love to put my mouth on you." Then that is followed by, "Are you at the cafe? I don't see you."

Sucking in a breath, I give a quick glance around. Unable to locate him, I respond with, "I'm here. We're in a booth today in the back part. Ethan invited Destiny so she could meet me."

A hand lands on my shoulder as I hit send and I jump, Benedict's laughter instant. "Scoot over."

Sliding in next to me, my phones barely clattered to the tabletop before he's got one arm around my waist, and his mouth on mine. His free hand roams, our tongues dancing as I try to orient myself to his sudden assault on my senses, moaning a little as he skims a hand down the front of my body. I'm exceptionally glad we're out of the sight of everybody else when he slips his hand underneath the hem of my skirt, which is knee length and more tight than loose, gliding the hand up my bare leg to the top.

As he moves between my legs, he pulls his lips away enough to whisper, "You've got about two minutes before they return to the table. Unless you want my hand to stay between your legs once they're here, you better come. And fast."

"I can't—"

He swallows my objection with his mouth, slipping two fingers inside me while using his thumb to tease my clit. I've never done anything in public, and so my nervousness at getting caught or someone hearing me wars with the desire furling through me at his expert touch. Inside me, he caresses my g-spot while on the outside his thumb goes around and around my clit, before passing over it in a series of quick touches, causing a shock of pleasure to shoot through me every time.

When he speeds up, I know I'm going to come around his hand, and it's going to be the quickest orgasm I've ever had, and I can't do anything to stop it.

But I think even if I could, I wouldn't, because this is so hot and it's the thought of him desiring me so much he'd do such a thing in public where we could be caught is what sends me over the edge. My small cry is lost in his mouth as my body tightens, my pussy clenching down on his hand, while the arm around my waist holds me firm in his grasp.

He embraces me for only a few moments before removing his hand. Releasing my mouth, he makes sure to catch my gaze and once he has, lifts his hand to his mouth and sucks his fingers clean of the evidence of what he's done to me.

"Yum." He gives me a naughty wink and a peck

on the lips. "Gotta get back to work. See you later, Caroline."

Seconds later, he slides out of the booth and out of my sight, vanishing so quick it's as if he were never there.

Leaving me sitting at the table with a flushed face and kiss-bruised lips as Ethan and Destiny return. Sitting across from me, Ethan busts into laughter the moment he looks at me, and after a look of confusion to him, Destiny's innocent eyes dart to mine.

"What's so funny?"

This makes Ethan's amusement grow and I mock scowl at him, the corner of my mouth lifting in a smirk. "Shut up! You're just jealous."

"Fuck, that was fast," Ethan says, sobering even though his eyes dance with glee. "Seriously. Where did he go? I should get some tips from him."

"Tips about what?" Destiny pokes him in the arm, demanding answers. "From who?"

He leans down to whisper in her ear, and I pick up my phone right as it receives a text message, feeling my face burn as I read the new message from the man who'd just gotten me off in the cafe.

"Sorry I had to run. Work keeps me busy. Can't wait to be alone with you again. That was just my hand. Imagine what I could do by adding my mouth to it."

Clenching my legs shut at the memory and the new rush of arousal thanks to my imagination, I type a quick reply with the only thing I can possibly say to that. "Looking forward to it."

"Oh, my gosh!" Jerking my gaze away from my screen, Ethan is smirking at me while Destiny's mouth hangs open. She snaps it shut only to end up opening it again. "You're dating Benedict? As in Miranda's Benedict?"

"Uh..."

She laughs at my speechlessness, clapping her hands together excitedly, and confusing the fuck out of me. I'm glad when she continues with whatever she wants to say. "Len told me Benedict met someone new, but he didn't tell me who. Said I wouldn't know her. Well I guess I do now, huh?"

With a nervous laugh, I nod at her, gathering she knows all about what's going on but not wanting to give too much away just in case. "Uh, I guess so. You know Len? I haven't met him."

"Know him?" She takes a sip of her soda, putting it back in place before stabbing at her salad with her fork. "Len's my brother. He's totally head over heels for Miranda, but he's a little nutty himself so..."

I don't think I should ask, or pry, or whatever. However, the opportunity to learn more about Benedict beckons me, and I've never been all that good at resisting temptation. So I don't, because Destiny is open enough I might end up learning something important.

"Doesn't dating your friend's girlfriend break a code or something?"

She shakes her head, answering me once she's swallowed her food. "Uh uh. Well, not to them I guess. Miranda and Benedict were together first, but I guess they all spent lots of time together, and Len's always had a thing for her. He never said anything though, 'cuz he respected Benedict and all, y'know?"

"So it was her idea?" I knew it was since Benedict has told me so, but I had no idea as to the extent of where her say began and his ended until now.

Laughing, she rolls her eyes, her fork mimicking her action in the air. "Everything's her idea. I mean, I've known her a long time and I love her, but she's got major control issues. Everything is her way or no way."

Something tells me that's the honest truth, and it makes me wonder why Benedict puts up with it since he doesn't strike me as the type of man to do whatever someone else wants. Either way, not really my place to ask.

When my phone vibrates, I look down at it only to notice the time, and slide out of the booth after grabbing my stuff. "Time to head back to class. See you two love birds later."

As they laugh, I walk away and open my messages.

"You smell and taste so sweet btw. Looking forward to more indeed."

I don't even reply, shutting the screen off and placing the phone in my pocket as I walk back to campus, sure the smile on my face will be permanent because my life is good and I know it.

CHAPTER TEN

Saturday rolls around before I see Benedict again.

Although we text a lot and talked a little on the phone, work kept him busy and studying for next week's winter finals kept me tied up, so I haven't seen him since those few moments in the cafe on Wednesday. Nathan's decided to spend tonight with Rissa, so when Benedict's text came through asking if I'd have dinner with him a few hours ago, I said hell yes with no hesitation.

He knocks on the door at five-thirty sharp, where I open it to find him 'dressed-down' from his usual suit and tie in khaki's and a dark green button-down. His eyes are quick to assess me in return from head to toe in a slow, appreciative manner, which he punctuates with a whistle.

Since he'd told me on the phone to make sure I

dress up, I'm wearing a strapless knee-length rose-colored summer dress, an ivory cashmere sweater in a nod to the cooler weather, and closed-toe matching sandals. I've pulled my hair back in a chignon and put in a pair of diamond dewdrop earrings my parents gave me for my birthday last year, but am not wearing any other jewelry because it's not something I like to do for the most part.

The look in his eyes when they meet mine once more tell me he sure loves what he sees and I step outside.

Closing the door behind me and locking it, he holds out his arm as I face him, so I take it. "Thank you."

"You're welcome." He leans in and gives me a kiss on the cheek. "Let's get in the warm car before you freeze and then I'll tell you how stunning you look tonight."

"Didn't you just?"

His happy laugh hangs in the air as we walk to the car. After I'm in, he walks around and gets in, then starts up the car and drives us away.

"You were saying?"

Using his left hand to control the wheel, his right hand sneaks over the center console and grabs mine, interlacing our fingers before giving them a gentle squeeze. "I said, you're absolutely stunning

Caroline. Anyone who sees you by my side will be jealous."

"Yeah, they'll wonder why such a handsome man like you is with a plain girl like me."

"Shut up." His reply is as teasing as my comment and he lifts my hand to kiss the back of it.

"Hey! No stealing my phrase."

"I'm older than you so I had it first." Opening my mouth to object, it's not long before I snap it shut again since he's technically correct, and he gives my hand another kiss. "In all seriousness, thanks for accepting my invitation to dinner. After the week I've had, you've made it much better with your simple presence."

"Are you kidding? I'd never pass up a free meal."

He lets go of my hand as he turns into the parking lot after winking at me. "I didn't tell you you were paying? Oops."

"Only gonna happen if they've got a dollar menu, buddy."

Pulling up to the entrance, he comes around to open my door, and once I've stepped out he tosses the keys to the valet. Once inside the hostess greets us with a smile, two menus in hand.

"Mister Grant, we've reserved you and your lovely guest a private room as requested. Please follow me."

"A private room?" My voice is a whisper as I lean into him while we walk behind the hostess. "Planning to take advantage of me in public again, *Mister Grant?*"

He grins down at me, wiggling his eyebrows, but not able to say anything as we approach the area reserved for us. The hostess opens the door and steps back, motioning us inside with a sweep of her arm. And once we're seated, Benedict orders wine and they leave us all alone.

"A girl could get used to this," I tease, pursing my lips for a moment when he looks at me, then drop my eyes to the menu when he gaze drops to my mouth. "I've never been here before so I need to see what they have."

"Sure, take your time. And Caroline?"

"Hmm?"

"That's the hope. That you'll get used to this," he clarifies when my gaze returns to his gorgeous, intense one. "Which you will, if you spend a lot of time with me."

"For now." Closing the menu, I lean a little forward in a conspiratorial manner, and speak in an exaggerated whisper. "You might discover I have terrible eating habits like consuming so much food you go broke. Or perhaps you realize I chew with my mouth open and chomp like it's going out of style."

Our waiter returns right then, and after Benedict taste tests the wine and approves, our glasses are poured. Once our orders are taken, the waiter exits as quietly as he arrived.

"You forget I've seen you eat, Caroline." His lips quirk as he holds up his wineglass until I follow suit. "To our new relationship and chewing with our mouths closed."

A snort of laughter escapes me and he smiles at my amusement before taking a drink of his wine. Setting down his glass, he holds out his hand in expectation, palm up. Switching the glass to my other hand, I don't even hesitate before placing mine on top his. He turns it over so my palm is exposed, and caresses the sensitive area with his fingertips along with an occasional stroke of his blunt nails.

Perhaps it's the memory of the moments in the cafe, knowing what his hands are capable of doing, but his gentle touch causes an instant reaction all over my body. My nipples perk up, straining against the bodice of my dress, while the surge of arousal between my legs has me crossing them in attempt to diffuse the feeling.

He knows what he's doing to me though, I can see it in the glint of his eyes and the curve of his lips.

"So," he says, continuing to stroke my palm

while his face grows serious, "our messages back and forth have been amusing, but we haven't really discussed anything serious since we met. Tell me about yourself, Caroline."

He's right, and while I understand him wanting to get to know me, it's been nice to just have fun and not worry about everything else. So I haven't because it would come in time, as it is now. I answer him with a mischievous smile. "What do you want to know? Didn't you think to stalk me on social media beforehand?"

"Nah." He sits forward as I had earlier, his grin widening even as he continues his subtle assault on my senses. "Part of the joy of meeting someone new is getting to know them in every way. If I know everything, you may cease to fascinate me before we fall in love with each other, and we don't want that, do we?"

What he says is so casual, yet I know the words are anything but. It's a promise of where we'll head if we keep this up, and at this rate, we're going there full speed ahead. "Guess I shouldn't admit I googled you, huh?"

"No need to admit it, I figured you had. It's a smart thing for a girl to do every time."

With a laugh, I tug my hand from his and he lets go without mention. "Girls are serial killers too, y'know. How do you know I didn't have or don't still have secret plans to destroy you. Hell, or murder you?"

"Look at me," he says with a sweep of his hand down his body, followed by him pointing at me, his amusement at this conversation crystal clear. "And look at you. I'm not afraid of you in the slightest. Next to me, you're like a little fairy; one flick of my wrist and you'd go flying."

With that imagery now in my head, I laugh out loud. "Shut up. I'm not *that* tiny, *Benedict*."

Eyes darkening, he opens his mouth to say something but is cut off by the arrival of our dinner. There's a whole lot of shuffling and hustling around, but when they are near to done, he says, "Please leave us in private until I ring. Thank you."

And just like that, it's just us again.

Alone. For as long as we want without interruption it seems.

My body's instant violent arousal at this knowledge has me crossing my legs and gulping down a gasp from the sheer surprise of it. He lifts a brow at me while digging into his food, the smirk he gives me right before taking a bite tells me he knows exactly what's going on with me, and he's loving it. Reveling in how he makes me feel.

Before taking another bite, he nods at my plate. "Dig in. You'll need the energy for later."

"Well, in the case..."

And there it is. The companionable silence falls between us while the sexual undercurrent is clear yet waiting to burst forth, counting on one us bursting the dam and letting our desire run wild.

It's me who does the setting free when we're both finishing up and I push my chair back a little. His body tenses, ready to pounce at my word, his eyes watching me with hot intent.

Knowing it was intention to have his way with me here, I suddenly feel brazen enough to give us both what we want and inform him with a wicked grin, "There's nothing under my skirt."

Beyond that, neither of us say another word as we move from our chairs to the floor like two first-timers who can't keep their hands off one another no matter how hard they try.

It's among the hottest sex I've ever experienced and to say it was mind-blowing wouldn't be an exaggeration.

But as I'll soon learn, it's true that what goes up must come down, and what goes around comes around, and all that other stuff we think will never touch us.

Because when one person isn't truthful, it fucks it up for the rest of us.

And by the rest of us, I mean me.

CHAPTER ELEVEN

"You need to tell me about yourself now since you distracted me earlier."

We're lying naked in bed at his house, where we returned to after dinner since we agreed to spend the night together.

I'm warm and comfy cuddled up next to him when he asks the question, and I give a happy sigh as I jokingly reply, "I'll tell you anything you want to know...just not where I hide the bodies of my scorned lovers."

With a squeeze of his arm around my shoulders, he chuckles softly. "Do you mess with everyone like this or am I special?"

"Hmm. Special, but only in that I mess with you more for some reason."

"Been told my whole life I'm easy to tease."

"*To* tease?" Lifting my head, I catch his hot

gaze with my amused one. "*You're* a huge fucking tease all on your own."

"How am I a tease when I always follow through on my promises?"

Giving him a wicked smile, I trail my hand I placed over his heart down his chest, but he's fast and catches it, shaking his head.

"Tell me about your family," he says, putting my hand back where it was and covering it with his own. "Or should I start instead?"

"Yeah, you should." I don't say it out loud, but I love hearing his voice, and I want to go off what he says rather than share something randomly.

"All right. First, you should know I never do anything like I'm supposed to. At least, that's what my parents have always said. They said I did my own thing and they let me, and it worked for all of us. Second, they've been married forty years, and I always thought I'd have the same terrific relationship they do. They weren't afraid to show when they weren't happy, but they showed me what a real relationship is all about.

My father's a lawyer, and up until a year ago, my mother taught first grade. And since you stalked me on the internet, you know I graduated high school a year early at seventeen, completed my Bachelors in three years instead of four, and graduated from law school. But it didn't take long in the real world for me to decide it wasn't what I wanted to do with my life. I opened up *Club Play* with a little help from my father when I was twenty-five."

"How does one go from law school to opening a club? Wait. Let's amend that to *three* clubs."

"It started with one and I simply fulfilled a desire students had in this area for a club that wasn't run down. One open more than closed at that. And now it's your turn."

"Hey, I already knew half that. Not fair."

He laughs, waiting until I give in with a sigh, resting my head in the crook of his arm.

"I'm not that interesting. I'm an only child. My parents met when they were both thirty, got married two years later, and I was born ten months after the wedding. They were well off and gave me everything I ever wanted and needed. Now they spend most of their time traveling since I moved in with Nathan and I see them about twice a year in person.

The rest of the time they video chat me from wherever they're at, and my conversations with my dad are short while my mom reminds me every time we talk that I need to live a little and there's no need to rush into anything with anyone. Even though I'm not engaged or anything, she says living with him when I can afford to live on my own doesn't make sense at my age. And of course, I'm still in college after graduating high school at the top of my class."

"What's your major anyway?"

My lips curve up as he kisses the top of my head. "Business Management. Next semester is my last meaning I'll graduate in three years instead of four, like you."

"And what will you do after that?"

"I don't know honestly. I've no student debt thanks to my full scholarship. And no other debts either. I can do whatever I want, and I know I'm lucky to be able to even have that option thanks to my parents, so I feel ridiculous not knowing where I'm going from here."

"You'll figure it out. You're twenty-one with your whole life ahead of you."

"Yeah, yeah. That's what my dad says. He's the laid back one and says if I'm gonna do something, make sure first and then do it right like he did. No need to make dumb mistakes even if I can afford to."

"Agreed."

Silence falls between us but it doesn't last long as I ask something I've been dying to since Destiny's comments the other day. "So, you introduced Ethan to your girlfriend's boyfriend's sister?"

"You must've met her if you're asking me that which means you know she's perfect for him."

"Yes," I agree with a laugh, "she honestly is, and he's already head over heels for her, but you didn't strike me as the matchmaking type."

"I'm not but I wanted to get you alone. And it worked." He pauses, then says, "But that's not why you asked me that, is it?"

"No."

He sighs, giving my hand he's covering with his own a squeeze. "It's okay, I figured she'd end up saying something eventually. Yes, Len is my best friend, and yes, he's been in love with Miranda for years."

"Why'd you do it? You said it's because she wanted to and you finally gave in, but why? You said you thought you'd have the same great love like your parents do, but..."

"Because I love her, and him. He seems to make her happy in ways I don't and haven't in a while."

There's something in his voice when she says that, but I'm not sure I should push my luck by asking how long ago the while was. Instead I ask, "Do you think she loves him more? They seem to spend a lot of time together. I haven't seen you with her all that much."

Pulling his hand away, he's quick to move until

I'm under him and he's staring down at me, eyes locked on mine as he's brutally honest. "Yes, I do, but that's my fault. Six months before her suggestion that we open the relationship up, she came to me saying she was pregnant."

My mouth drops open, my eyes widening at the casual way he says this, and he continues with a grimace.

"She caught me off guard. We'd always been so careful, so when she said it, the first thing to come out of my mouth was, 'but I'm not ready for a child.' She didn't even give me a chance to process it before storming off in tears after telling me 'too bad.' Didn't talk to me for weeks and I apologized to her many times following it, telling her I truly was excited. And I was once I'd gotten used to the idea. We might've been okay if she hadn't miscarried at ten weeks. She's never forgiven me for what I said after that."

"Oh, Benedict..." My eyes fill with tears at his obvious pain as he glances away. "Is that why you gave into her?"

His gaze returns to mine, his eyes blazing. "Yes. And honestly, if it had to be someone, I'm glad it's Len. I know he will never hurt her and will protect her as I have."

Because it echoes what Frank told me at the bar

the first night, I raise a brow at this. "Protect her? From what?"

"Herself. But that's not my business to share. However, no matter what's between us, I love her, and she's the type of person that something has to be her decision. So if she wants us to end, she'll choose it, and she hasn't." With a soft kiss on my lips, he asks, "What about you? Why did you agree to an open relationship?"

"Oh. We were open from the beginning after Nathan made it clear that's the type of person he is. I accepted it because I liked him a lot and wanted to get to know him."

"You were seventeen. That's pretty open-minded for someone of that age, isn't it?"

Shrugging, I wrap my arms around his neck and smile up at him. "Yes. I suppose most girls my age would've been, but I dunno. I guess I never felt like I owned a person; like they had to be mine and only mine for our love to count as real. I've never questioned his love for me because he's never given me a reason to. And for the first three years of our relationship, we actually were only with each other. Didn't plan it, was just the way it worked out until he met Rissa."

"It's a misconception that an open relationship means people sleep around indiscriminately. I never imagined I'd find myself in one, but I've never thought badly of the concept itself."

"Yes, it is. He only sleeps with me and her. And he was my first."

Bringing his weight down on me, I wrap my legs around his waist as he returns my smile. "I'm your second? Now *that* I didn't know." His eyes practically twinkle as he lifts his body up a bit and slides his hands between my legs. "How'm I doing?"

My response comes in the form of meeting his lips with mine, making it so there's no more words between us, just touch.

It's all the answer either of us needs in this moment.

CHAPTER TWELVE

I take my last winter final on Thursday morning.

As I'm walking from the campus to my car, a text message from Benedict comes through, bring an instant smile to my face.

"You coming to see me after you're done?"

I love how he's so eager to spend time with me. He's had a bit more time to text and talk this week, but we haven't seen each other since Saturday. He's promised to cook me a 'thank fuck the semester is over' dinner tonight at his place.

"Yes," I reply once inside my car and have shut the door. "Starting my car now. I'll be there soon."

"Excellent. I'll still be in a meeting once you arrive, but wait for me in room 2 in the back. I'll join you asap."

Not bothering to reply, I toss my phone on the passenger seat and once my cars warmed up a bit, I head to see him. Finding a parking place is easier at this time, especially since it's more of a bar and grub place until seven at night every day, and Frank smiles from behind the bar when he catches sight of me.

"All done for the semester?"

"Yep." He's got a glass of soda waiting for me on the bar before I even reach it and I pick it up while returning his smile. "Thanks. I'm just gonna wait for Benedict in room two like he said."

"My pleasure."

Turning away as he starts to wipe off the counter, I walk through the door leading to the private for pay area of the club, and down past the employees break area. I've only been back here once when Benedict took me into his office the first night, and while it's not big enough to get lost in, I'm glad I took everything in that time.

Knowing room two is at the end of the hall, I am about to walk past room one when I hear raised voices.

And I stop cold at realizing the female is Miranda.

I should keep walking. I shouldn't eavesdrop and I know it. But just as I'm about to continue on down the hall, a male voice says, "We have to tell Benedict."

And like an idiot begging to get caught, those

words have me stepping closer to the door to hear better.

"I know, I know. But it's hard. I love him."

"I don't want to share you anymore baby. This has been going on long enough. You know I love him like a brother, but we both know you two aren't good for each other like you used to be."

"Len." Her voice is wobbly and it sounds to me as if she's been crying. "He did this for me because he loves me. How can I betray him like...like... you know it's bad enough we started before he even agreed."

Son of a bitch.

My hand covers my mouth just in time to prevent them from hearing my gasp, and I step back from the door as quietly as I can, feeling sick for Benedict the whole time. I'm still able to hear them though as Len replies and makes everything ten times worse.

"Baby, he doesn't know that and it doesn't matter now. But you're gonna start showing soon and it's better to tell him before that." It's quiet for a moment as my mouth drops open, then as she sobs, he says, "Come here. Don't cry. It'll be okay."

I don't know why I continue to stand there, but all I can think is what assholes these two are. My relationship with Benedict might be new and we're more in lust with each other at this point than anything, but I already care about him. Through our talks and the time we've spent together, it's also clear he's a good man, and to know these two were messing around behind his back has my stomach roiling in anger.

It's made worse by the fact I now possess information he deserves to have, but I don't know if I'm the one who should give it to him. And I'm pissed off at myself for having stopped to listen because I've put myself in this position.

Shit hits the fan as my phone rings in my pocket and the door to room one flies open in an instant, the male version of Destiny stepping into the door with a glare at me.

"What the fuck are you doing?" Len's words are angry, but the look on his face makes it clear he knows I heard everything they said.

Miranda walks up next to him, swiping at her eyes before focusing on me, causing her lip to wobble as tears threaten to fall again. "Oh god, Caroline. It's not—"

"Don't waste your breath. It's clear she heard the whole fucking thing," Len mutters with an angry wave of his hand in the air before pointing at me. "Get out of here and keep your mouth shut."

My back straightens with indignation at his audacity. "Excuse me?"

He takes a step toward me, and I take one back,

but Miranda stops him with a hand on his chest. "Len, calm down. She won't say anything. Right, Caroline?" She keeps her eyes on me and waits for me to agree.

I never get the chance to rip into her like I want to.

"What's going on here?"

At the sound of Benedict's voice, I watch as Len steps back into the room and takes Miranda with him, shutting the door behind them. The touch of Benedict's hand on my shoulder causes me to jump and whirl to face him.

"Caroline?" His eyes fill with concern as he steps real close. "What's wrong? Why are you crying?"

"I am?" A touch of my hand to my cheek shows me, yes, tears are sliding down my cheeks and it's evident I need to get away from here right now. "I... I gotta go. I'm so sorry."

Then, before he can stop me, I duck under his arm and dart past him, fleeing the club while hoping a little space will show me what the fuck I'm supposed to do.

And give those two idiots time to come clean before I'm forced to tell Benedict myself.

CHAPTER THIRTEEN

Honesty is the best policy.

Even as I avoid Benedict with lies, I still believe this.

And I hate lying. I despise it.

I'm a terrible hypocrite for hating lies, yet giving him bullshit excuses as to why we can't get together.

It's that time of the month.

The weather is making me sick.

My cat died.

No, I don't have a cat here. It lived with my grandma.

Yeah, the cat belonged to my grandmother. The only thing making it better is it's clear he knows something isn't right because it's been a whole week. He keeps asking me what happened, what did Miranda and Len say to me, am I okay?

No. No. As a matter of fact, I'm not okay.

I remember their conversation, I know what Benedict told me, and I wonder if she made everything up when they were together to get her way.

If he feels guilty for nothing.

And here I am, not telling him what I know, and I'm wrong. I know I'm wrong, but I don't know if telling him is the right thing to do either.

He's my business, but I have to figure out if that includes his relationships with other people, and the things I hear about them.

The sudden ring on my computer, indicating I'm being called, jerks me out of my thoughts. Seeing it's from my mother, I answer and her face — so similar to mine that I'm sure of what I'll look like in thirty plus years — pops up on the screen. Her smile is big and happy, and so contagious I find myself reciprocating.

"Hi, Mom."

"Hi, honey! You doing all right?"

I'm not sure why she always asks me that. One time I said no, and went to tell her why not, and she ended up having to go in a flash. So I don't even bother anymore. "Yeah. How're you and Dad? How's London?"

"Lovely, darling! Your father and I are

thoroughly enjoying ourselves. How'd finals go? Did you get our gift?"

I finger the well-fitted diamond bracelet they sent me, holding my arm up so she can see it. "I did. Thank you again. I would've called you but never saw you online—"

She waves her hand. "No worries. Should be us apologizing. We've been so busy we almost forgot your birthday! How terrible that would've been!"

Honestly, I wouldn't have cared, but she does so I laugh with her. "It's all right mom. I know you guys would never forget about me on purpose."

She winks. "Any plans for the holiday?"

Christmas is two days away, but Nathan and I don't have any plans because neither of us really celebrate it. In all the time we've been together, we've never bought a gift for one another — at my insistence. We would spend the evening together having dinner and watching a movie, but that's it. I'm not even sure what we're doing for New Year's now. We usually go to the club, but I'm avoiding that for obvious reasons.

"You know me, Mom," I say after a moment. "Never any plans 'til the last second here."

Maybe she knows something isn't right, because she just stares at me through the cam, pursing her lips as she studies me. But then the look is gone and she nods. "All right. Well, in case everything gets busy, Merry Christmas darling. Your father and I decided to just put the money we'd spend on your gift in your account so you can buy yourself something you want instead, okay?"

What I would love is to spend time with them, but no point in saying anything else except what I always do. Taking care of me is how they show their love and I know it. I accepted it long ago on the outside. "Okay. Thanks, Mom. Love you."

"Love you too, sweetie. Gotta go now, I'll give your father your love. He's out and about."

"Thanks. See you later."

Taking off the bracelet, I stick it in my purse. I only wear the things they buy me when I know they're going to want to see it. It's the one reason Nathan and I don't buy gifts for each other. He knows how much it bothers me, even though rationally I know he's not buying my love. I simply don't want to even feel like he is for a second.

I'm lost in my thoughts when the doorbell rings, and I end up ignoring it because I know Nathan will get it. And after a few minutes pass, I figure he took care of whoever showed up, but then he yells up the stairs.

"Baby, come here!"

Shutting off my computer, I head toward the steps and walk down them slowly. But seeing it's not Nathan wearing a suit along with a heart-stopping smile at the bottom of the steps has me halting and tossing Benedict a glare. Without a word, I whirl around and start back up with a stomp.

"Stop." Benedict doesn't raise his voice, but his command is firm and full of authority, enough so I want to turn around and flip him off.

Ignoring him, I continue walking and seconds later, it's clear he's following me as I knew he would. As I want him to with everything in me. And with that little admission, I take off with a dash because I don't want to face him.

Fuck, I don't know why I think I can beat him, but I try. Making it to my door, I'm almost inside when he picks me up from behind and carries me into my room, kicking the door shut behind him.

He holds me to him with one arm around my body under my breasts and it's in this position where his power and strength are clear. No matter how much I thrash about, he simply carries me as if it's nothing, his breathing easy and even.

"If you think this is off-putting, it isn't." He chuckles and my heart quickens as he carries me toward the bed. "I love a passionate pre-fuck fight as much as I love someone letting me do whatever I want while they're not moving. Either way, I'll enjoy myself."

God, at those words alone I remember the way

he fucked me on the table, and admit in my head how much I'll enjoy what he's about to do too. Going limp in his arms, he places me so I'm facedown on the bed, and I don't even fight him.

"I wanted to talk first, Caroline," he says into my ear after covering my trembling body with his rock hard one. "But you don't want that do you? Would you like me to fuck you like we both want me to first?"

Afraid to speak because of the words I don't want to say just ache to fly out of my mouth, I use my body instead. Lifting my hips a little off the bed, I grind my ass into the front of him, the feel of his hard-on stroking the flames between us, and a moan of need escapes from both of us.

"Good fucking choice."

There's no hesitation in his touch, and he doesn't take the time to get either of us completely naked. He moves off me, yanks down my bottoms to my feet where I kick them off, protects us both, and well, there's no other way to describe it. He impales me with his cock in one delicious, self-assured thrust, my body hanging over the edge of the bed with my legs straight.

"Oh, god!" The cry is ripped from my throat because while I wanted it, I wasn't completely ready for it, and it hurts enough to make my whole body tense up.

"Do you want me to stop?" He pauses, his tenuous hold on his self-control evident as he grips my hip with one hand, and with a fleeting thought I wonder what his other hand is doing.

With a shake of my head, I keep my head down even as I slide my arms straight, fisting the comforter in my hands as I wiggle my hips to encourage him on.

"Good." He pulls to the edge, teasing us both as he lingers there, and plunges back in hard enough to make us both gasp. "I'd stop if I have to but I don't fucking want to."

Every single thrust after is followed up with a question or statement, and I stay unresponsive while the overwhelming pleasure thrums through even in spite of the fact he's pissed at me. For some reason, his anger turns me the fuck on, and every single word he speaks sends me closer and closer to the edge of my first orgasm since the last time I saw him.

"What the fuck is wrong with you?"

"You can't just have sex with me and then fucking feed me bullshit excuses."

"Was going to wait on you, but I said screw it. Decided I'd just fuck it out of you instead."

And on and on, until I feel his hand slam down beside me on the bed, the other leaving my hip to slip between my legs and stroke my clit just right.

I come hard, seconds before him, my mind going blank while my body shakes beneath his, and with a final thrust, he joins me. Both of us go limp, his body resting on mine, and he presses a soft kiss on my shoulder.

"Caroline?"

"Hmm?" My eyes are closed and I'm just enjoying the feel of having him close, wondering what the fuck I'm going to do when he starts asking questions. I'm hoping he doesn't ask me right now because I'm not ready.

But he doesn't. Instead, he says, "I crushed your chocolate chip muffin."

I can't even keep my eyes from popping open then, looking to where his hand had slammed down beside me, and there is the muffin he brought me. The muffin I hadn't even seen him holding.

With that, laughter bubbles up and out of me.

Followed by tears as I burst into sobs at the realization I have to do the one thing I don't want to.

CHAPTER FOURTEEN

"Why do you have your own room?"

Benedict's question comes after he's comforted me while I cried, stripped us both naked so we could shower, and followed it up by climbing into bed with me. Well, after he cleaned off the muffin mess he made.

Now we're cuddling under the blankets. I'm half lying on top of him with my head on his shoulder, one leg thrown over his waist, and the other palm-flat over his heart. It won't be long until he'll ask me what's wrong again and I'll have to tell him, but for now I answer his random question.

"Easier to sleep for both of us. Nathan snores louder than I like, and I apparently move around too much, sometimes kicking him. I guess one time he was on the edge of the bed and he fell off 'cuz of me."

"I know that all too well," he says, voice filled with amusement as he presses a kiss to the top of my head. "You're also a blanket hog."

"Am I? You were under them when I woke up."

"Yeah, after I fought for them. Twice. You've got quite the grip on everything involving me even when you're doing nothing else except sleeping."

There it is. The catch in his voice, the one which makes it clear my behavior hurt him when all I wanted to do was the exact opposite.

Taking an unsteady breath in, I let it out slowly and as he squeezes me in a show of support, I say, "You're a good man, Benedict."

"But...?" When I don't continue, he sighs and disentangles his body from mine, sliding away to sit on the edge of the bed, head in hands. "I'm not stupid, Caroline. I know something happened. They said something to you and you just need to fucking tell me what the hell it was."

Sitting up, I hug my knees to my chest, the ache of the last week back in my chest. "I...it's not what they said to me, but what I heard."

"And?"

"I'm not sure it's my business." When he turns enough to look at me, my emotions threaten to fall from my eyes in the form of tears at the grim line of his lips and the burning disappointment in his gaze.

"I was just trying to avoid having to tell you before they did."

"Well, they didn't. So, tell me."

Shaking my head, I hug my knees tighter. "Why don't you ask them? You should hear it from—"

"No." He cuts me off with an angry swipe of his hand in the air, his voice rising. "Tell me now, Caroline, or this is over. You're with me, so you owe me your loyalty. If you can't tell me anything, how will I know you won't keep things from me? Especially when it's coming between us!"

"But, it's not that simple—"

"Bullshit." He cuts in again, crawling close to me again, enough I can feel the heat and anger radiating off him in waves as he lowers his voice to a dangerously deceptive level. "If they're deceiving me, I deserve to fucking know. Do you think I wouldn't tell you if I overheard Nathan and Rissa talking about something I'm pretty sure you weren't aware of? Because the shit has to be pretty bad if you're avoiding me over it."

I flinch, not because he's angry and his words cut into my heart, but because he's right. Yet it's the step Len took toward me after telling me to keep my mouth shut that keeps replaying in my head. What would he have done if Miranda hadn't stopped him? Would he do anything at all if I do say something? Maybe he'd just been upset someone had heard and wasn't trying to threaten me?

"Caroline, it's impossible to avoid getting hurt in any relationship at some point. I'm asking you to divulge what you heard even if it hurts me." He lifts a hand to my face and gives it a brief caress with the pad of his thumb. "I'm a big boy, sweetheart. I can take it."

Averting my gaze as tears cloud my eyes, he drops his hand as I give him what he wants, but say it so soft he leans in to hear me. "I overhead Miranda saying they started before you agreed and she's... uh, pregnant."

His flinch is unmistakable. His sharp intake of breath is like a shot in the silent room; whatever he expected me to say, it wasn't that. And I can't look at him, because I'm not sure I won't break down crying for him. The silence stretches on and on, and I feel the need to say something. Anything.

So I try to comfort him. "Maybe the baby isn't his? Maybe—"

"Not mine," he interjects with a cough. "Not possible unless it's the longest pregnancy on the fucking planet."

"What?" Although the urge to cry is still there, my mouth drops open while managing to meet his once again, and I snap it shut before continuing.

"He said she'll start to show soon. That's like, four or five months right?"

He glares at me, anger evident in the thin line of his mouth and tense jaw. Getting off the bed, he goes over to the window, shoving a hand through his hair as he stands there peering out even though I know he's not seeing anything beyond the glass.

"She moved out six months ago," he finally says. "We haven't had sex in eight."

Oh.

Ooooooh.

Hot fucking damn.

"Benedict... I... wow. I'm sorry."

"Why?" Turning away from the window, he regards me with self-mocking smile. "I'm the idiot who didn't see it coming. Scratch that," he says, lifting a hand up as I go to interject. "I saw it coming. I chose to fucking ignore it like a moron."

Not knowing what I can really say, I extend my hand to him, wiggling my fingers in invitation. "You could continue standing naked by my window calling yourself names, or you can come back to bed with me. What'll it be?"

His cock jumps at my question, making it clear which way his body wants to go. He stalks toward the bed, towering over me until I lean back on the pillows, and then he walks around the bed before getting in.

Lying on his back, he fists his cock, his eyes seeking mine out and finding them. "Straddle me." When I do, he keeps his one hand on his cock while using his free one to grip my chin and makes sure our gazes are connected before he says, "Thank you for telling me."

"As if I had much of a choice?"

"Of course you did." He swipes his thumb across my lips and when they part, he smiles. "It might've taken you a week, but you chose honesty when I made you face me."

"You brought me my favorite muffin and fucked me like you missed me. How could I not?" We both know I'm not serious. Yeah, I hoped she would tell him before I did, but in the end, I would've told him no matter what. And for that, I add, "I'm sorry for putting you off. You're right; I didn't want to hurt you. But that's not for me to decide when it's something you should know."

"Apology accepted."

"You don't seem all that surprised though."

"Your girlfriend doesn't stop sleeping with you eight months ago without it being clear something isn't right, Caroline. I wish I could say I'm surprised they began before she talked to me about it, but I'm not."

"Why...? Did you suspect?"

He drops his hand from my mouth, his smile

rueful. "No, I didn't, but there's no use in being angry about it, is there?"

"You're still gonna wait for her to break up with you even though she cheated?"

"I told you, it's the only way to go," he says with a shrug. "Did it sound like they were planning to tell me?"

"Uhm, he wants her to tell you, but seemed like she was afraid for you to find out the truth."

"I believe that."

I'm sure he does. It's clear he's given up on her, but I am still taken aback at his lack of what I think would be a proper reaction at what he's heard from me. "Are you hurt at all by this?"

"I stopped being hurt by her a while ago. Not much surprises me anymore when it comes to Miranda. We'll part ways when she says we will and I suspect it will be sooner rather than later now."

"And your friendship with Len?"

He lifts a brow at the same time as his hips. "Do you really want to continue talking about this, or would you prefer to ride my cock and give us something else to focus on?" Grabbing one of my hands, he replaces his hand with mine, and puts both of his behind his head. "Well?"

The fact he doesn't want to talk anymore is obvious. So, instead of answering him, I do what he least expects and scoot back a little before bending over and covering the tip of his cock with my mouth. His hiss of surprise is followed by a guttural groan, and his hands slipping into my hair, fisting it even though he keeps his grip gentle. Flicking my eyes up to his face shows his are closed, so I shut my own while taking him deeper until I can't go any further, my hand tight at the base.

It doesn't last long. I've never considered myself real good at it, so when he indicates with a light tug that I should stop, I do. His eyes are gleaming as they meet mine, reaching for and then handing me a condom.

"Much as I love having your mouth around me, sweetheart, I want you on top."

I'm barely into position when he grabs my hips and thrusts into me with a single, hard lift of his hips.

"God," he says, pulling me down so we're skin to skin, and hugs me close. "I'd fuck you all day long if I weren't such an old man."

"Shut up."

We both laugh and he releases me, letting me straighten up before cupping my breasts in his hands and squeezing them.

"Have I told you how much I love these?" He flicks his thumb over each nipple, making them rise and tighten as he grins. "Because I do. They almost overfill my hands, but not quite. They're perfect."

"They might be, but I'm not."

I don't realize I've said that out loud until he frowns, and slides his hands around me to pull me down toward him once more. He presses one, two, three soft kisses to my lips, then whispers against them.

"You don't need to be perfect. Just be yourself, Caroline, that's all I care about." A longer, deeper kiss, and then, "It hurt more to have you avoid me like that than what you told me. I'm never going to be mad at you for being honest."

"Okay."

He smiles against my lips. "And after this, I believe you owe me dinner."

"Mmm, I am hungry."

"I've changed my mind."

Don't even get to ask him what he means. He invades my mouth with his tongue, sliding a hand to cup the back of my neck, rolling us over until I'm on my back and he's surrounding me. There's no more talking, only sighs and gasps and moans during the gentlest sex we've had together yet.

CHAPTER FIFTEEN

The answer to my question about his friendship with Len is answered the following evening.

Arriving at the club with Benedict hand-in-hand, it's only seven p.m. yet the place is packed. Benedict keeps it open tonight for Christmas Eve, but he'll shut down at three a.m. and won't open up again until the day after Christmas.

Walking through to the bar, it's funny how many people say hi and greet him by name, and I wonder — not for the first time — how the hell I never knew he was the owner. Guess that goes to show how much I didn't pay attention, but I sure am now.

I'm a little nervous tonight. I haven't seen Miranda or Len since that day, and I think Benedict somehow knows how I hope to avoid them, because he won't let go of my hand. He keeps me close until we hit the bar where we sit, and Frank greets me with a warm smile.

"Caroline, glad to see your lovely face, darlin'. What d'ya want to drink?"

"Hmm. Make me something tasty and pretty."

He winks. "Coming right up, I've got the perfect thing for you. Sir?"

"You haven't called me sir in five years, don't start now Frank." They both laugh and Benedict shakes his head. "Nothing for me right now."

A pair of arms encircling me from behind make me jump, until I hear Ethan's laugh and Destiny's distinctive giggle.

"Caro, you too busy being Ben's slut to call me?" he sits his head on my shoulder and when I turn my head a little to look down at him, he's pouting.

"As busy as you are being Destiny's prostitute. Where's my money?"

He laughs and lets go of me, sitting on the stool beside me as I whirl to face him. "In my back pocket. She paid me all in one dollar bills. You'll have to dance for it."

"Hi Caroline," Destiny sings, wrapping her arms around me without warning, or invitation.

"Uh, hi."

After I give her an awkward return pat, she

steps back with a grin, and throws her arm around Ethan's shoulder while he encircles her waist with his.

"No, really." Ethan's tone is serious now and he rests his free hand on my bare knee, eyes searching mine. "You okay? Your texts had me worried and I wanted to kick somebody's ass, but didn't know whose."

"I'm taking care of that," Benedict tosses in as he places his hands on my shoulders and bends to kiss the crook of my neck. "Speaking of, I'll be right back."

He walks away before I can respond and I crane my neck to see where he's going but soon, he's lost in the crowd.

"Here's your drink, Caroline," Frank says, catching my attention. "It's called purple haze."

"Wow, it's really purple!" Destiny notes with a giggle.

"Yeah, hence the name." Frank nods at me. "Let me know if you like it. If not, I'll make you something else."

One sip tells me all I need to know. "It's like drinking candy, Frank, and I love the color. Thank you."

"I'll have one!" Destiny shouts like Frank is deaf and he winks at me before walking away to make one for her.

"Caro—"

That's all the words able to leave Ethan's mouth before we hear a female scream and a man saying, "What the fuck man?"

I know the voice though, and with a 'watch my drink' to Ethan, I make my way through the crowd. It's pretty easy to shove my way through as people stop to gawk, and right as they all appear in my sight, Miranda glares at Benedict.

"What the fuck is your problem?"

Len is holding something to his face, blood drops on his shirt making it clear Benedict punched him dead square in the face. Miranda stands between them, although it looks as if Benedict retreated a little, and she glares as her focus shifts to me when she realizes I'm nearby.

"Oh," she says with a slightly hysterical laugh. "I get it. Turns out shutting your mouth isn't your strong suit, is it?"

"Lay off, Miranda, and go to my office," Benedict says as the music shuts off and people continue staring. "This isn't the place for private conversation, as you two should've realized last week."

"You started it by punching him in the face."

"Go, Miranda. You and him. *Now.*" He looks up at the DJ. "Turn the music back on. Sorry folks."

Benedict reaches me first, but it doesn't prevent

Miranda and Len from glaring at me as they walk by us on their way to the office.

We follow them, and seeing Benedict flex his hand, I ask, "Are you all right?"

"I'm fine. Can't say the same about his face."

I bite back a laugh at that. "Was it necessary to punch him the moment you could get close enough?"

"No, but it felt great."

As they reach the door and walk inside, I stop. "I don't need to be in there with you, Benedict. They sure as hell don't want me in there."

"Personally, I don't give a shit what they want, but if it makes you uncomfortable then stay out here. However, I need someone in there with me as a witness."

"To what? Murder?"

With a chuckle and shake of his head, his lips meet mine in a sweet kiss before he steps back. "If you don't want to go, how about Ethan? Destiny is Len's sister and Frank is loyal to me, so they're both out for those reasons. Have to protect myself."

"Okay, let me go ask him."

Of course, Ethan agrees after I give him a brief idea of what happened, and goes to join Benedict. It's not that I don't want to hear what they have to say, because I do, but I think it's better if I'm not in the room with them at all.

Unfortunately, that leaves me alone with a freaking out Destiny at the bar who asks me a bunch of questions and insists on wanting to go check on her brother. I'm not sure what I should or shouldn't say, so I just try to keep her as calm as possible while we wait and finish my drink, followed by another.

About a half hour after they go into the room, I receive a text from Nathan.

"I need you to come home right now. We need to talk."

Frowning at the vague yet urgent tone of his message, I send back, "Okay. I've had two drinks though and I didn't drive. Come get me?"

"K, be there in ten."

Waving at Frank, I wait until he's close to say, "Looks like I gotta go. I'd text Benedict but I don't want to interrupt him. Let him know Nathan needed me at home and came to get me okay?"

"Of course. Merry Christmas, Caroline."

"You too, Frank. Keep an eye on this one." Turning to Destiny after he nods, I tell her, "Stay here and wait okay? Be calm. I'm sure they won't be in there much longer."

Not even waiting for a response, I make my way to the front door, which takes a bit as the club has even more people than when I arrived barely an hour ago.

By the time I get out front, Nathan is waiting in the car. Once I'm buckled in and we're on the road, he says without even glancing over at me, "I need to go on a trip tomorrow morning."

"What? To where? For what?"

"Work needs me to fly to close some deal across the country. I could be gone anywhere from three days to a week, depends on how negotiations go, but they want someone there in person."

"Oh... okay."

I'm not sure what else to say in the face of his matter of factness about the whole thing, not seeming to even care they want him to go on Christmas day, and my heart plummets as I look out the window. We've always spent the whole day together and now we won't get to. Yeah it's his job, but couldn't he go the fucking day after? Seriously.

"... somewhere else to go?"

Focusing back on him, I frown at what I did catch of the sentence. "I'm sorry, what?"

He sighs, covering my hand with his as he turns the corner toward our home. "I said, I'm sorry it's such short notice and that I'll miss Christmas with you. But, I don't want you to be alone, and we've never been apart like this. Leaving you alone in the house by yourself worries me. Will you be okay?"

"Yeah, I'll be fine. I'm not afraid of empty houses. Besides, it's not like I don't have anybody to call to come hang out with me." Turning my hand over under his, I lace our fingers together. "I'm glad we can spend the evening together at least."

"I wish I didn't have to go," he says, kissing my hand before releasing it. "Come on. Let's go inside where it's warm and make the most of the night."

Once inside, we get ready for bed and as Nathan puts a movie in as is the tradition, my phone buzzes like crazy. I send both Ethan and Benedict the same message without reading what they said: "Can't talk tonight. Nathan going on trip in the morning, spending evening with him. Talk tomorrow."

I don't know what they say, because I put the phone on silent, and snuggle up to Nathan as he returns to my side. It's not long before I fall asleep.

And when I wake up in the morning, he's gone.

CHAPTER SIXTEEN

I text Ethan at ten a.m. and it's not long before he arrives at my house eager to fill me in on the details of last night. We're barely sitting at the table eating the breakfast he brought before he's talking a mile a minute.

"We get in there and Miranda gets all nasty, asking him what I'm doing in there. And when he says he needs witnesses, she freaks out asking him what he thinks they're gonna do. He says 'besides what you already have been doing and are doing' and she didn't like that. He sat behind his desk after saying that, and I just kept standing by the door. They were both sitting on the couch. Len looked like shit but he wasn't bleeding anymore."

"Did he break his nose?"

Ethan makes a slicing gesture in the air. "You

know better than to interrupt my stories! But no, he's fine although he kinda deserves it huh?"

"You tell me, mister story teller."

"It was bad, Caro. Benedict asks her if there's something she needs to tell him, and she starts crying like the manipulative bitch she is, and Len got all defensive. He's like, 'oh we were gonna tell you, just trying to find a way' and Benedict said, 'you mean you were gonna tell me how you were fucking Miranda before we opened our relationship?'" Ethan laughs at his own memory and rolls his eyes. "Len's like, 'oh I thought you were talking about her being pregnant.' I about died at the 'you're an idiot' look he gave Len.

"Then he tells Miranda to stop crying and say what she needs to say so they can all get on with their lives. Of course she cried harder while telling him she was almost five months pregnant and it was over between her and him because she wants to marry Len. Benedict said finally, now both of you get the fuck out."

My mouth drops open. "You're exaggerating."

"Of course I am. We were in there a long time, a lot of other dumb shit was said by those two, but it's not important. They tried to justify what they did by saying they wanted to make sure they would work out before she left him. Uh huh. He wasn't believing it either."

"Poor Benedict. He deserves better."

"Yeah," Ethan agrees with a scowl. "Poor him. He needed comfort, too, yet comes out to find you gone. Frank told him Nathan came to get you for something not even ten minutes before, and he understood, but didn't look happy about it."

My phone buzzes and Ethan gives me a knowing smile before finally digging into his food.

Of course the message is from Benedict. "Good morning. Are you alone?"

"No. Ethan is here. Sorry I had to leave like that last night. You okay?"

I poke Ethan in the arm while waiting for Benedict to answer. "Where's Destiny?"

"With her parents. She'll text me when she is free to get together."

"You two spend a lot of time together."

Buzz.

"Yeah, we do. She's awesome."

"I'm happy for you."

Buzz.

"I know you are. Answer him before he shows up at the door and drags you back to his cave by your hair, and so I can eat in peace."

Rolling my eyes, I pick up my phone and read what he's sent.

"Not really, but I'm sure Ethan filled you in. It's over. They said they're going to get married. I may or may not be drinking." Followed up with, "Any chance you can come over?"

"He wants me to come over. Says he may or may not be drinking."

"That means he's probably drunk."

"Strange reaction for a man who told me he stopped being hurt by Miranda a long time ago."

"Caro, don't be an idiot." When my mouth drops open at that, he uses two fingers to shut it and gives me a disapproving look. "He might've known her breaking up with him was inevitable, but it doesn't make it hurt any less no matter what he tells himself. I mean, they're getting married *and* having a baby. That would hurt anyone who loved someone who didn't want to be together anymore after eight years together."

"Yeah, you're right, I guess. I know I'd be pretty upset. If I go, will you drive me over?"

"When you go, you mean? Yes, I will take you."

I text Benedict back with a sigh. "*Yes, I'll be there in a little while.*"

His reply is instant. "Good. I need a hug."

And just like that, my heart melts. I would need a hug too, but not sure my biggest reaction would involve drowning my pain in alcohol. However, I'm not him and I barely see him drink, so I'll let him do it his way as long as it doesn't get out of hand and comfort him the best I can.

"Sooooo." Ethan raises a brow at me, unable to speak since he's chewing. "When you going to your family's for dinner? Are ya taking Destiny?"

"Usual time and no. I guess Len and Miranda are planning to tell his parents all their bullshit so it's absolutely necessary she's there." He says the last few words with immense sarcasm and rolls his eyes. "Merry Christmas to me. I told her she'll meet everybody at New Year's though, so she's pretty excited."

"You two are pretty serious."

"Says the girl with two boyfriends?"

"I would say touché, but I've yet to meet either of their families, and I like it that way."

His head rears back, eyes going wide. "What? You've been with Nathan for how many years and you haven't met the fam? That's not cool, Caro."

"It's no big deal, especially since I don't want to meet them, and I told him so."

"Why? After all this time they probably think you hate them, or you're a snob."

"Guess I'm a snob then."

"Caro..."

I don't need to explain it to him because he already knows, but every so often he thinks he has to try and make me admit I hate my parents for not being around. I refuse to say it because there's so much more to it than that and I'm not engaging with him today, so I shake my head. Then, with a huff of irritation, I grab my stuff off the table and throw it away, turning to head toward the steps once that's done. "Just drop it. I'll go get ready and we'll leave in like... ten minutes?"

"Yeah," he says in a strained voice. "I'll be waiting in the car."

I don't even turn back to look at him before heading upstairs and barely a minute passes before the door slams behind him as he exits.

CHAPTER SEVENTEEN

I send Benedict a text minutes before we arrive at his house, and Ethan waits while I walk up to the front door and ring the bell.

The second the door opens, I'm staring at a half-dressed drunk and grinning like a fool Benedict, and it's not much longer before Ethan speeds away. But I'm not paying attention to that; all my focus is on the gorgeous bare chest in front of my eyes.

Oh, and the overwhelming scent of liquor.

He steps back, extending his arm in invitation with a flourish, which causes some of whatever he's drinking to slosh over the rim and onto the floor. Shutting the door behind me and locking it, I step toward him with my hand out and he frowns at me.

"You don't need that now that I'm here."

He hasn't said a word to me yet, and I start to wonder how much he's had to drink, even though he isn't showing any signs of intoxication. The downturn of his mouth becomes more pronounced as it equals the pain in his gaze, but he places the glass in my hand with a curt nod.

I set it down on the table by the entryway, take his hand in mine, and say, "Let's go lie down."

He's like a puppy, following me without question with his hand tight on mine, and I know he's drunk for sure now. The fact he hasn't said anything, not one word, has me worried. His demeanor, which is usually lively and commanding, is subdued and...well, heartbroken I guess. It's possible I could lead him to a slaughterhouse right now and he'd let me, which is fucking terrible.

As we enter his bedroom, I'm wishing I could punch both Miranda and Len in the face for what they did. Shit, for what they're still doing. Anger at the way they've treated him when he loves them both boils inside me, seeking an outlet even though I don't have one, and I stomp it down like I've had practice doing for so long.

I'm so lost in my thoughts I don't notice Benedict's let go of my hand until the door is clicking shut and I jerk back to the present as

Benedict grabs me. Whirling around, he imprisons my body against the door, and I wrap my legs around his waist. He seizes my mouth with his own as it opens on a gasp, his actions leaving me in a desperate bid for air after he steals my breath. It's not even a split second before his tongue swoops in and gives me no rest, tangling and toying with mine at the same time his hands find my wrists and he's raising mine above my head, holding them there with a strong, firm grip of one hand.

My body responds while my brain tries to catch up, his now free hand slipping between us and underneath my skirt, pushing aside the silky material of my panties and slipping one finger followed instantly by another inside me. I whimper into his mouth as he strokes me just right, getting me nice and wet until I'm sure I'll have no issue taking his cock into my body, and his hand leaves just as quickly as it arrived.

"Fuck, I'm sorry," he mutters against my mouth before invading it again while I feel his hand fumbling between us to undo his pants. I count *one, two, three* before he moves the fabric aside once more and the head of his cock is pushing inside my pussy. He grabs hold of my ass, his voice raw and gravelly, and full of desire as he drags his lips away to speak. "I need you. I can't wait."

He slams into me, swallowing my cry with his mouth once again while thrusting into me over and over, so fast I'm not even sure if I'm breathing anymore. However, I feel everything even as my arms go numb from the way he's holding me, as if all the feeling in my form is floating toward where our bodies are connected.

I've marveled on his strength before but the way we're standing, the way he's holding me, and the way our bodies match perfectly even at his pace is nothing short of amazing to me. The hand gripping my ass keeps me angled in a way I'm protected from hitting it on the wall and getting bruises, yet I know I'll feel the effects of this tomorrow.

When he releases my arms with no warning, they fall to my sides as if I'm a rag doll, and his hand slides down until it's squeezing my other ass cheek. He rips his mouth away, resting his forehead on my shoulder, but if I even think for a second it gives me a chance to say something, it doesn't. His new hold gives him extra power to lift me as he draws out before entering again, the long hard strokes hitting me just right when he yanks me down, over and over.

"God, Caroline." He moans into my neck, pressing rapid kisses up and then down it as his grip tightens to an almost painful level. "You feel so fucking amazing. You always feel so fucking incredible."

I don't know what it is about what he said, but my eyes fly open at realizing what we've done. What we're doing, with no fucking protection, but it's too late. The words to tell him to pull out on the tip of my tongue get stuck as my orgasm rolls over me swift and strong, my fingers digging into his shoulders while my whole body tightens all over and around him. With a final thrust he comes, his fingers holding onto my ass as if it's a lifeline, a long throaty moan emerging from his mouth as he stills.

I shove at his shoulders. "Let me down."

He doesn't respond and I'm about to repeat myself when he finally lowers me to the ground, making sure my feet are touching the carpet before releasing me with a frown. "What's wrong?"

"We broke the rules, that's what's wrong."

I can practically see how what I've said sends his sluggish thoughts whirling, going through the rules to see which one we possibly broke, and the subsequent widening of his eyes as it hits him.

"Shit!" He steps away from me and glances down, then back at me with a mixed expression of horror and disbelief. "I didn't mean—I'm clean—"

Holding my hands up palms out, I interrupt

him. "Stop. I'm on birth control, we're both clean. That's not the point and you know it."

He stares at me until the insane urge to wiggle as if I've done something wrong shoots through me, and then he shoves a hand through his hair and shrugs. "Well, go on and do whatever you've gotta do now that we broke the rules. Actually," he says with a quirk of his brow, "what're you supposed to do if this happens?"

"Tell him." I whisper this, and I'm not sure why, but he smiles as if he finds this funny.

"Really?" He laughs. "Well go ahead then. Text him and say, 'Merry Christmas, Benedict was drunk and forgot to use a condom while he fucked me against a door while I was fully-dressed. Sorry!' But you'll have to call for a ride if you need to go home now, since I can't drive." As my mouth drops open, he whirls and stalks off to the bathroom, slamming the door.

I pull out my phone, yet I'm hesitant to send a message to Nathan. Benedict didn't do it on purpose and it wasn't like I wasn't at fault, too. Not really sure why he suddenly has an attitude about it, though. The rules have been clear from the beginning.

Marching after him, I stop in front of the bathroom door and smack my palm against it a few times before yelling through to him. "No need to be a dick, Benedict!"

The door flies open and he glares at me. "Stop shouting."

"Stop being mad at me for—"

"I'm not mad at you; I'm *furious* with Len and Miranda. As for right now, I'm fucking annoyed." Lifting a hand to his head, he rubs his palm right above his left eye as he speaks softly, the pain back in his voice. "And I have a headache. I need to lie down."

He turns the light off and brushes past me, shedding what little clothes he's wearing on the way until he's naked, and then climbs into bed. I go into the bathroom and clean up. I'm not in there longer than five minutes, but when I come out he's snoring and I've no desire to lie down next to him right now.

I go back downstairs to find something to do only to end up discovering copious amounts of liquor bottles, making it evident Benedict's probably been drinking since last night and hadn't slept at all until now.

For the first time since Frank warned me about Miranda, I wonder what the fuck I've gotten myself into while acknowledging it's too late for such a thing.

Especially since I'm falling in love with him,

which means even if I do tell Nathan what just happened, I'm not sure I'll break up with Benedict if he wants me to.

And just like that, the lines around the rules blur, and I'm not sure what the right thing to do is anymore.

So, in the end, I don't say anything at all.

CHAPTER EIGHTEEN

"Who are you when nobody's looking?"

Benedict's question is random, coming out of nowhere really, as we sit on the couch later in the evening. The TV isn't on, he has the fireplace going, and we're simply enjoying each other's company along with some delicious wine.

After cleaning, I went into the living room and laid on the couch while watching TV, but must've passed out. It was six p.m. when Benedict woke me, having just gotten up himself. After a kiss and an apology for earlier, he made dinner, and what happened wasn't mentioned.

I don't know if he thinks I messaged Nathan and doesn't want to ask to avoid pissing me off or something, but I don't bring it up either. At this point, it doesn't matter really, because I want to keep him as much as I want to keep Nathan. And for me, that means letting a little slip up go, because I know he didn't mean to forget, and I'm not blameless.

"Um," I answer when he gives my shoulders a squeeze, bringing my attention back to the present. "I'm always just me. I don't pretend to be something I'm not."

"Never? Not even to impress someone?"

"No." He lets go of me as I sit up and set my glass on the table, then snuggle into his side again. "I often thought my parents put up a front as I was growing up. Doing whatever they needed to try to fit in, to make sure I fit in, and they weren't true to themselves. They tried to buy my love like every other parent they knew did with their children."

"Is that why you don't like gifts?"

Pulling back a little, I stare up at his face in surprise. "How did you know I don't like getting gifts?"

"I didn't," he answers with a grin, setting his glass on the table as well before shifting me to straddle his lap while facing him. "Lucky guess after realizing just now how you didn't receive any birthday gifts. Problem is..."

"Is?"

"Well." He grimaces, lifting his hips a little to dig into the pocket of his lounge pants, and pulls his hand out, clenching whatever it is in his fist. "I bought you a Christmas gift."

My stomach drops, along with the smile from my face, but he prevents me from getting up with a strong hold on my hip.

"You should see what it is before you freak out." His grin is playful even though his eyes are serious. "I'm not trying to buy your love, Caroline. Or even your like. I saw it and thought of you, that's all."

"Benedict..."

"You might hate it and dump me," he teases, giving my lips a soft kiss as he holds up his hand. "Do you want to see it or not?"

I hate how hopeful he looks while we sit here, staring at one another, my heart racing as if I'm being chased. It's just a gift; an innocent token of affection. It shouldn't hurt, shouldn't burn my chest the way it does as the anxiety weaves its way around inside me, yet it does. I want to see it at the same time I don't.

Years with Nathan and I've never let him buy me a gift, but he's also never offered one out of nowhere. He took me at my word that I didn't like receiving them and so as to not upset me he's never bought me one. But what do I do in the face of being presented with a gift by Benedict, who bought it simply because it made him think of me?

Shifting my focus to his hand, I notice I can't see anything, which means whatever it is, it's small.

He moves it to right in front of my face, murmuring as his burning gaze holds my anxious one, "If you don't want it after you see it, it's okay. I'll understand. But you should at least look. It won't bite you."

I square my shoulders and give him a nod. "Okay. Show me."

Opening his hand, a thin silver necklace hangs from his index finger, and I follow it down until my eyes land on the item dangling on the end.

A little silver muffin-shaped charm.

My lower lip wobbles while my eyes fill with tears at the thoughtfulness of the gift and when I lift my gaze back to his, he frowns. "No? Should I have gotten the one that said 'eat my muffin' instead?"

His question sends me into a fit of unexpected laughter, which he joins in with, and after they fade away I throw my arms around his neck, burying my face in the crook of his warm, naked shoulder. His arms embrace me without hesitation, one around my waist while the other cradles the back of my head, and he chuckles.

"Guess this means I'm not gonna be dumped for buying you a present?" When I shake my head but don't lift it back up, he laughs again. "Let me put it on you then."

"All right." Once I'm sitting up, I take both of my hands and lift up my hair so it doesn't get snagged in the clasp of the necklace, and as he puts it around my neck, I ask, "What about you?"

He slides his hands down to my shoulders once the necklace is on and smiles at me. "What about me what?"

Dropping my hair, I snatch up the muffin charm in one hand and roll it between my fingers while staring at him. "Who are you when nobody's looking?"

"I'm like you; I don't like to pretend. I'm the same whether someone is looking at me or not."

"So you don't have any deep dark secrets?"

He glides his hands down until they rest on my bare thighs, one on each side with palms down, and toys with the edge of my skirt. "No. I think you do though."

"I don't!"

With a flick of his wrists, he tosses the skirt up, baring me to his eyes for only a moment before covering me once more, and laughs. "You do with these skirts. I've never seen you in a pair of jeans. You're always wearing a skirt. Do you even own pants?"

"Other than pajama pants? No, but that's not a

secret." I think he expects me to say of course I have jeans and such, but I don't. So when his eyes widen and his mouth drops open, I shrug and explain. "My mother always dressed me in skirts, even when I was a kid. I never, ever wore jeans or yoga pants or anything like that. Then, I went to all-girl schools up until high school, but even then, the uniforms had girls in skirts. I suppose it's habit more than anything else now."

"Well, it's a hot habit. Every single time I see you, all I can think about is how easy it would be to bend you over and fuck you with little to no effort." Trailing a finger on the soft skin of my inner thigh, he slips his hand under the material, and then between my legs where he discovers I'm not wearing panties, which has his soft smile turning into a wicked grin. "Or, like right now, discovering you have nothing on under that skirt makes me want to lift you into the perfect position and thrust into you so fucking hard you scream."

Other than the grin, he's looking at me the way he did the day I saw him across the cafe, and my body's instant arousal has me involuntarily clenching my legs, which I know he feels because the hand on my thigh contracts a little as if he's trying to control himself. With the hand between my leg, he keeps all but one finger still, sliding it between my labia, spreading my wetness around before slipping the digit inside my pussy as deep as he can go. It's not long before he has two fingers in me, and his thumb is manipulating me on the outside.

He uses his other hand to bring us close as we can be with me sitting on his lap, and I drop my forehead to rest on his shoulder, closing my eyes to enjoy the pleasure he's giving me. I feel him reaching between us, sure he's freeing himself, and take a quick peek to see that's exactly what he's doing.

Then, I feel him turn his face to the left, his lips brushing against the top of my ear, which he takes between his teeth and nips a little. The bite is followed by him sucking on it, then licking around the edges until I shiver, and he removes his hand from my body, leaving me feeling empty.

It doesn't last long. I feel his cock probing at the entrance to my pussy, but he doesn't go in. Instead, he stops and groans, his voice deep as his fingers dig into my hips. "Will you break up with me if I fuck you without anything Caroline? Tell me you'll break up with me or I'm not going to stop. I've always used protection, earlier today was the first time I never... god, you felt so fucking good."

I admit, I'm shocked. So surprised at his admission I don't say anything and he starts talking again.

"It's just you for me, sweetheart. And I know it's the rules, but fuck the rules. You're my girlfriend, too. Can't we make up our own fucking rules?"

"Benedict—"

He lowers my body, his cock entering me a little bit more, and a streak of pleasure makes me whimper, cutting off what I was going to say. He practically growls his words into my ear now, wanting his answer. "Are you going to break up with me? Yes or no?"

I should. Earlier I could blame on him being drunk, but now he's asking me to blatantly ignore the rules. And making me choose. It should be black and white, I should climb off and say it's over, but I can't. No, I can, but I don't want to. I'm caught and I've no wish to escape, no matter what the consequences are.

Because here, in front of him and in his grip, and not alone, I'm still me. I won't pretend I don't want this and I won't pretend I don't know what it might do. We're looking at each other and we see everything we want, and everything we need, and everything we shouldn't be doing.

Earlier we stepped over a line and we shouldn't have. We should stop, but we don't. Instead we're going to keep on walking right past the line as if we didn't see it.

"No," I finally whisper, giving into my desire over my rationality, and that's all he needs.

He yanks me down hard while thrusting up into me and makes me scream just like he promised while I fall in love with him a little more.

A phone ringing jolts me out of a deep sleep the next morning.

Well, afternoon technically, as the time on my phone when I pick it up indicates it's twelve-thirty. Seeing it's Nathan, and Benedict continues sleeping soundly next to me, I slip out of the bed and into the bathroom before answering.

"Hey."

"Hey baby. Did I wake you?"

"Uh, yeah, it's okay though. How was your trip? You didn't text me."

He yawns, the sound loud enough I need to move the phone away from my ear until he's done. "Exhausting. I didn't get much sleep. Sorry I didn't say goodbye yesterday, I didn't want to wake you up. How was your day?"

"Oh, um, it was okay."

My own statement makes me wince, especially when he doesn't say anything right back, as if he's trying to find something in my voice. Which, of course, he does because we just know each other too fucking well.

"Are you all right, baby? Did something happen?"

"I uh... I spent the day and night with Benedict. Miranda and Len are having a baby, and she... well, she broke up with him."

"Shit."

"Yeah." I pause, biting my lip while my brain screams at me with my own guilt. *Tell him*, it shouts.

"Anything else bugging you?"

I start to wonder if he's able to read my mind, or if the way I'm acting is a dead give away I want to tell him something. Then I realize I'm sitting naked in a bathroom I went to so I could speak in private to my boyfriend in my other boyfriend's house. I'm an adult, I can do this, and I know it's the right thing to do.

"Benedict and I are pretty serious, Nathan."

"Yeah, I know. Just like me and Rissa. I'm happy for you."

"It's... it's different Nathan. You know, from me and you? I didn't see it the way you said you did the other day, but—"

"What?" There comes the change in his voice, from laid back to alert, as if he's waiting for some bad news. "Is something wrong?"

"No, well, um, maybe. Look—"

"Nathan," a woman's voice says in the background. "Where's my—"

Her voice cuts off and Nathan says, "What, Caroline? Sorry." I hear a door shut and he continues. "You know my secretary, she came with me. What were you saying?"

Yeah, I know his secretary. I didn't hear her well enough to know if it was her, but now I'm angry. "Your secretary? You didn't tell me she was going with you."

"We work together, baby. She goes with me everywhere business related." He sounds impatient and I hear a drawer slam before he speaks again. "Now, what's wrong?"

"Benedict was drunk yesterday when I arrived and didn't use protection." I spit out the words, which is not how I wanted to deliver the information, but I think my own guilty conscience is putting trouble where there is none.

There's a huge, pregnant pause after that and I would think he's hung up except for the sudden slamming of another drawer. Out of a need to say something, I add, "And I didn't notice until it was too late. But then—"

"Stop, baby. I'm not sure what the problem is here or why you sound so upset about it."

It's one of those moments where my head jerks back like I've just been smacked in my face and can't believe it."Uh, what?"

"You're on birth control. He's not sleeping with anyone else, is he?"

I can't help but blink in rapid confusion as my brain tries to wrap itself around his calm question. This isn't what I expected at all. "No, just me, but the rules...?"

He laughs, and all the sudden, his voice is back to its normal laid back sound. "Wow, you really took those literal, didn't you baby. No need to sound all terrified I'm gonna be mad. I'm not like that. I thought he hurt you or something for a moment."

Now I'm really fucking perplexed. "Nathan...?"

"You two are together, not just having casual sex. Protection is necessary if you're just getting to know someone, but if you're both clean and he's not having unprotected sex with anyone else, why in the world would you think I'd be upset?"

"Oh...wow. I'm...so..." A tear I didn't know was there slips down my cheek and I sniffle. "I felt so fucking bad last night because we did it again and... and—"

"Baby, calm down. You've got a severe guilt complex going on. Perhaps it's time you saw your counselor again?"

"No." It comes out with a huff attached to it. "A rule is a rule, that's what I was always taught. And the first time was on accident, but later it was a choice, and in the moment, I didn't care what you thought."

"Good for you, baby." His voice is back to being curt as he slams another drawer and I wonder what the hell he's doing. "You're not a robot, for fucks sake, and I don't own you or your choices. Whatever you decided is fine." Another pause. "Look, I gotta go now, got a meeting soon."

"Well... okay then. Do you know when you'll be back?"

"Not yet. Love you baby. Talk later."

He hangs up before I can respond and I lower the phone, shutting it off as I stare at it like I just finished having a conversation with an alien. I'm not sure how long I'm sitting there, but I jerk my head up when the door opens.

Benedict leans against the frame and crosses his arms while lifting a brow in question. "What're you doing in here?"

"Nathan called and I didn't want to wake you up by sitting there talking."

"Ah," he says, holding a hand out to me. "I was

about to say my bathroom is clean, but it's not really a place you wanna just hang out, is it?"

I stand up with a shake of my head, and slip my hand into his. Leading us back to the room, he takes the phone out of my hand and places it on the nightstand before lifting me and placing me in the center of the bed. Lying down, he pulls the blankets up to cover both our bodies, and curls his body around mine so I'm trapped.

"Want to tell me why you looked like somebody killed your non-existent cat when I came into the bathroom?" My groan at his reminder of my excuses only makes him laugh and with a soft peck on my lips, he says against them, "Seriously, tell me."

"And if I don't?"

"Then I'll have to beat you."

"Ooh, I'm scared now."

"Caroline..."

"Benedict..."

"How old are you again? Twenty-one?" He chuckles, snuggling me closer as I give in to a small laugh of my own. "You told him, didn't you?"

"Yeah... and he didn't give a shit, basically."

"Well, I'm sure that's a relief." The fact his body relaxes next to mine makes it obvious he was at least a little worried himself. "Seems you thought he'd be pretty upset, so why aren't you pleased he doesn't care?"

"I am. Relieved, I mean."

He readjusts until he is leaning on one elbow and looking down at me, eyebrows lifted in question. "But...?"

"There was a woman with him. He said it was his secretary. I didn't hear much; either she didn't know he was on the phone and stopped talking once she saw, or he cut her off."

"You think he's cheating?"

"No." My answer is instant, but not completely true, and I frown at my own uncertainty. "I don't know. It doesn't fit him. I mean, I have no reason to doubt him, at all."

"A bit of a severe reaction to just hearing a woman's voice. What else happened, Caroline? I know you're more rational than this."

My lips wobble then, my watery gaze caught in his increasingly kind one. "He was rather abrupt with me, as if I were annoying him with my worries. He went from normal to... to that, and I stared at my phone like that after because it was like... well, I was stunned. He seemed like he couldn't get off the phone fast enough."

"So, I need to kick his ass when he comes back, is what you're saying?"

"No... no, I don't think so. I've no reason not to

trust him. He said he was tired, maybe he really had to go. I don't want to jump to conclusions, but..."

"But, you can't help it because you've never been apart like this."

"Yeah." I smile up at him and slide my arms around his neck. "I think that's part of it. And my own little issue with last night. I think it's all getting to me."

"Let me take your mind off of it then." He lowers his head, brushing his lips over mine once, twice, and cups my breast in his free hand as I open my mouth to let his tongue explore inside. It's a slow, lazy dance of seduction, and it might've gone further if my stomach hadn't chosen to growl.

Chuckling, he drags his lips away, the hand on my breast sliding down to rest on my belly while grinning down at me. "Guess what you really want is some food?"

"Raincheck?"

His answer isn't verbal. Instead, he bends over the bed, picks me up, and tosses me over his shoulder.

He tortures me by tickling my feet all the way to the kitchen, and I pay him back a little later with a tiny surprise called whipped cream when he turns his back on me like a moron.

CHAPTER TWENTY

L ater in the evening, Benedict has to go to work, and I join him.

When we arrive, it's pretty quiet. Frank's the only other person there, so when Benedict goes into his office to deal with some things, I take a seat at the bar.

"You here for the whole day, darlin'?"

"I'm here for as long as he is tonight," I reply with a wink. "Make me the drink I never got to finish the last time?"

"Coming right up." He grabs a glass, working his magic as I sit there and watch, then sets it in front of me with a smile. "On the house. Enjoy."

"Oh no." With a shake of my head, I hand him the money for it. "You have to let me pay."

"Nope. Benedict said you get drinks for free."

Seeing the scowl on my face, he shrugs and holds out his hand. "How 'bout you just make it a generous tip and we'll call it even?"

"Deal." Slapping the ten in his hand, I say, "Keep the change."

After sliding it in his pocket with a grin, he leans in real close as I take a sip of my drink and whispers, "How's he doing?"

"How much do you know?"

"Enough to wanna give Len a matching shiner on the right side of his face."

"I can't believe Benedict punched him. Didn't strike me as the physical type of guy."

"Nah, he's not really. So?"

"He was drunk the next morning but I went and took care of him."

"I bet you did."

"Perv." When he chuckles and steps back, I roll my eyes and take a few more sips of my drink, before smiling at him. "I think he'll be just fine. He's hurt, but he saw it coming, and so did you."

"I hate to say I told you so..."

"Shut up, no you don't. You might not've wanted to be right 'cuz you care about Benedict, but you're happy to tell *me* you were spot on."

"Yep."

He turns away to continue setting up, so we fall

into a comfortable silence while I drink, and after a little while I decide to speak up again.

"Did you have a nice Christmas, Frank? Spend it with your family?"

Tossing me a smile over his shoulder, he nods before turning back to his task. "Yeah. Me, my five sisters, and my parents had a blast. You?"

While shocked to learn Frank has five sisters, it's nice to learn a little bit about him, and I share what little I can with him. "Nah, my parents are in London. Nathan had to go on a work trip, so I spent the day with Benedict."

At that, he turns, brows lifted together in obvious surprise. "Really? Did you go with him to see his parents too?"

"No." Finishing off my drink, I sit the glass down with a grimace. "Wow, that's really sweet at the end."

"Want another?"

"Mm-mm, not right now." He takes the glass, turning to the back counter as I ask, "Was he supposed to go see his parents?"

"He usually goes on Christmas day. But I suppose if he was drunk, he wouldn't've been able to drive anyway."

Interesting. I don't remember Benedict being on the phone at all, and wonder if he called them the night before to tell them what happened. At least, in general, not specifics. I decide I'll ask him about it later, and tug my buzzing phone out of my pocket, where there's a text from Ethan, who must've finally gotten over our little discussion the other morning.

"Hey. :) How's it going? How's the boy toy? Did you have a nice Christmas?"

The fact Ethan still calls Benedict my boy toy is amusing, since he's older than both of us and Nathan. "Everything is fine. I'm at the club chatting with Frank right now while he works. How was yours?"

"*Yeah,*" he replies almost instantly. "All good. Destiny and I will be there later. :P Save me a dance?"

"Of course."

"Good. And sorry about the other day. They're your relationships, I don't have a right to tell ya how to deal. You know I get it even if I disagree."

"Yeah, I do. It's okay. :) Love you, see you later!"

"Ditto."

"So," I speak to Frank's back as I put my phone on the counter with a soft tap. "Tell me about this family of yours. Five sisters and no brothers in sight?"

"Nope. And I'm the youngest."

"Ah, I get it now."

He turns with a quirk of his brow and amusement tugging at the corner of his lips. "What do you get?"

"Why you're single."

I'm clearly teasing him, and he knows it because he laughs and shakes his head. "I'm single because I'm always at work, and am not interested in meeting girls who frequent clubs. I like me someone who's a computer geek, that way I know they'll always be at home."

"You know how you find a girl like that?"

"How?"

"Online dating."

His facial expression changes from interested to 'no way in hell' as he shakes his head again. "Nope. Not gonna happen."

"Why not? I did it. That's how Nathan and I met, actually."

"Because I don't trust people on the internet. Bunch of liars and fakes."

At that, I laugh, giving him a pointed look. "Because people who meet under regular circumstance like in a bar or in college like Benedict and Miranda did are always honest and real?"

He holds up a finger, opens his mouth, and shuts it before glaring at me. Then, he does something extremely juvenile: he sticks his tongue out at me for a second before saying with a laugh, "Fucking logic doesn't belong here. Get away from my bar."

"I love you, too. How about another drink for me and whatever Benedict usually has. I'll take it to him."

He winks and does as I request, and a few minutes later I enter Benedict's office after giving a soft knock. He doesn't look up from his work, where he has a pen in hand and a pencil between his teeth, as I approach. Once at his desk, I set the drinks down as gently as I can, and walk around until I'm standing next to his chair.

I know he knows I'm standing there, but I like how he pretends he doesn't realize I'm here. It gives me a chance to study him. His hair is ruffled like usual, but more than normal, which means he's probably been running his hand through it. The spicy and sexy scent of his cologne mixed with the clean ocean scent of his shampoo from the shower he took after the whipped cream fight teases my senses, making me wish we could have sex right now.

Well, I know we could, but I don't want to disrupt his work. So, I bend a little and lean in, pressing a soft kiss to his cheek. I intend to do that, take my drink, and go sit on the sofa, but he seems to have another idea. In a reaction I probably would've found impressive were I not trying to catch my breath, he slicks an arm around my waist, pushes his chair back, and plops me into his lap with a chuckle. I take the pencil out of his mouth and toss it away, not caring where it lands as he gazes down at me with a grin filled with naughtiness while I lie across him, my legs dangling over one arm of the chair.

"I wasn't trying to disrupt you. Just wanted to bring you something to drink and give you a kiss."

"I know." With one arm supporting my back, he moves the other to rest on the bare skin between my knee and the edge of skirt, caressing it as he shuts his eyes while tipping his head to rest on the back of his chair. "I just couldn't resist touching you."

"You don't ever have to refrain from putting your hands on me."

"Glad to hear it. But, in that case, what must I refrain from if not touching you?"

"Mmm. Nothing."

"Carte blanche is dangerous, Caroline."

Him and using my name! Giggling, I tease him in return. "Is it, Benedict? And why's that?"

"Because it means I can do anything and you'd

be up for it. You wouldn't stop me. What if I did something you don't like?"

With a shake of my head, I finally move so my arms are around his neck, and my tongue darts out to give him a quick lick on the lips. As his lips twitch in reaction, my head falls back as I bust into laughter, and say, "Not possible. Sometimes I think you know me better than I know myself."

"I don't," he admits, shifting underneath me so his increasingly hardening cock rubs against my ass through my skirt and panties. "I just know myself and am certain we are alike in many ways. Possibly more than you even realize."

"Probably."

His mouth inches closer to mine. "Almost certain."

"Within an inch of potentially and for sure."

"Smartass." His hold is firm on my hips and he grinds into me. "Caroline?"

"Hmm?"

"I'm cashing in my raincheck." He shifts me with those words, until I'm bending over his desk and he's behind me pulling down my panties, making me step out of them.

"But somebody could walk in!"

"Guess next time you'll make sure to lock the door just in case." His statement is followed up with a slap to my ass and thrusting into me so hard and sudden the desk moves a little, enough to make us both laugh. "Ah, fuck."

That's the last of the talking for a good bit.

Oh and nobody walks in on us.

Whew.

CHAPTER TWENTY-ONE

Three days have passed since Nathan called me the other morning, and he hasn't called me even once. He's texted back in response to my texting him, only to tell me he's busy and he's sorry. Oh, and he loves me.

Yeah, I love him too, but he's starting to piss me off.

I realize I'm probably having a complete overreaction to him being gone because it's never happened before, and yeah, it's not healthy. Blah, blah, blah. I don't care. I miss him and it doesn't seem like he misses me at all.

Maybe if classes were still in session, I would be too busy to notice or care so much, but they aren't. I'm not busy. I'm spending most of my time with Benedict which is great because I love being able to learn about him and spend so much time together, I truly do.

But I want the man I've been with for almost four years now to hold me, and kiss me, and make love to me the way we both enjoy it. I want him to call me so I can hear his voice because not talking to him is making me so fucking sad.

I've never had to miss him like this, but it hurts. I didn't know it could hurt this much, and part of me wonders if this is how Benedict felt when Miranda started spending more and more time with Len. I'm understanding his desire to drink, even if I won't do the same thing because it's just not the type of person I am, even if it's not the same kind of circumstances.

If it were? God, I'm not sure I'd handle it all that well. Losing Nathan would be...it would devastate me, make me feel a way I've never felt and don't want to ever feel; I know that much.

What makes it worse is the fact I'm starting to feel the same about Benedict, and that's even scarier. We haven't been together for what anyone would consider a good amount of time, yet I'm falling for him hard. He's just such a sweet, kind, and wonderful man all around; everybody loves him.

Well, okay, maybe not Len and Miranda as

much anymore, but all his employees think he's the best. And I can see why. I've spent pretty much all my time with either him or Ethan and Destiny, who are usually hanging around here now since it's the holidays, and gotten to talk to all the staff in one form or another as well as see him in action.

He talks to all of his employees with complete respect, never has to reprimand anyone, pays them well above minimum wage, and gives them all the schedules they prefer. It's clear why this place is the place to hang *and* the place to work in town, especially if you're a college student.

A place I'm in right now, sitting at the bar nursing a drink, as Benedict's in a late meeting with a vendor. Frank's been casting me worried side glances, and I'm sure it's due to the frown I've had since showing up earlier this evening. When he finally gets a break, he heads toward me, and leans in so I'm the only person who can hear him.

"You all right? You look upset. Whose ass do I need to kick?"

"No. I am. And nobody's right now. Just missing Nathan."

"He's still not back?"

I shake my head, a tear slipping down my cheek as my emotions slip through, which I wipe away with an angry swipe as I say, "It's New Year's Eve the day after tomorrow. We've never been apart during Christmas, let alone New Years. We barely speak too and it hurts. I wouldn't care if he talked to me more."

"Sorry, that sucks. I'm sure he's just busy. Maybe you gotta just keep busy too. Spend time with Ethan or Benedict or hell, even me. I'm glad to have you around. You want something to do maybe to take your mind off of it?"

"Like what?"

With a glance over his shoulder, he follows it up with an amused grin. "Wash those dishes for me?"

Pursing my lips in consideration, I ask, "Anything else I can do?"

"Well, I need the whole place swept and mopped once it calms down, if you'd like to do that instead."

Shaking my head, I laugh and stand up. "Dishes it is."

About twenty minutes pass and when I'm almost done with washing, I see Benedict approaching from the side and turn off the water right as he throws his arms around my shoulder with a naughty grin.

"Ready to get out of here?"

"Pretty sure you've got a few hours left 'till close, don't you?"

"Yes, but Frank's closing up tonight so we can spend some time together while I'm *not* also at work." He turns me and tugs me against him, lowering his head to nip at the lobe of my ear before whispering into my ear, "See? I do learn from my mistakes, which means making time for my woman no matter how busy I am."

"Yeah?" Tossing Frank a smile of thanks, I slide my arms up Benedict's chest until they are wrapped around his neck and my smile widens with happiness. "Well then, let's dance."

As he scowls, I tilt my head toward the dance floor and give a soft laugh.

"Come on, just one." Stepping up on tiptoe, I brush a kiss across his lips and follow it up with another laugh. "And then we'll go back to your place for some naked horizontal dancing."

"Sounds like a terrific idea, although I wish we could skip out on the dancing."

"Even if it means you'll get all hot and bothered before then by me rubbing up against you?"

His eyes grow hotter at what I've said as we head to the dance floor. Just as we arrive, the song changes from a fast-paced dance to a slow love song. Benedict doesn't waste time pulling me close, our bodies swaying in tune like we've done this a million times, and kisses the top of my head as it rests against his chest. Neither of us speak, just simply enjoying how close we are to one another, and even though the club is packed, it doesn't feel like we're surrounded by others. All I see and feel is him, and in this moment, he's my whole world.

Lost in my thoughts, it takes me a moment to register the fact one of his hands slipped from my waist to ass, while the other found its way between our bodies and I smile as he starts fondling the charm on the necklace he bought me.

"I love the fact you haven't taken this off since I gave it to you."

"It makes me feel close to you even when you aren't around."

"Good." He removes his hand and puts it back around my waist. "Means when school starts up again, you won't forget about me when you're busy."

"Ha." A lift of my head has us gazing at each other, our happiness reflected in the other's eyes. "As if I would."

"I know I'm hard to forget about. I think about myself all the time too."

My lips quirk. "Shut up, Benedict."

"Make me, Caroline."

"Okay."

Wrapping my arms around his neck tighter, I jump into his arms and he catches me with a chuckle, which gets lost when our mouths meet.

There are a few cat calls from those around us while we stand there, my legs wrapped around his hips while he holds me steady with his hands on my ass, but I barely notice. In this moment, I'm free, happy, and not caring I'm in a public place. And when our lips separate for a breather, he lets me slip to the floor as he says, "Home, now."

A suggestion I'm all up for because all I wish right now is that we were naked and in bed together. But just as we turn to walk toward the door, Benedict stops, his eyes narrowing at whatever he sees over my shoulder.

"Fuck." Lifting his hand in a signal I've recently discovered is meant to get the attention of the security team, he gives me a quick kiss and says, "Hold that thought. I'll be right back."

He walks away once I nod and with a sigh, I head over to sit at the bar to wait. Not even two minutes pass though before the security team is hauling two men into Benedict's office and he's returning to me with a scowl.

"Sorry, but I've got some shit to deal with. Was hoping it wasn't what I thought, but looks like someone's been pushing drugs in here for a while now." My mouth drops open at this disturbing turn of events while he grabs my hand and lifts it so the palm is up, then places two keys in the center of it and closes my fingers around them. "Take my car and go to my place. I'll be there soon as I can. Make sure you turn on the alarm like I showed you. Frank'll bring me home when we're done for the evening."

"What? No. I'll wait for you—"

"Caroline, please." With a kiss on the top of my head, he looks over at Frank and says, "Make sure she gets outside and into my car safely, man."

"Yep. Go deal with those morons."

While I hate that he won't let me stay, I sigh as he looks at me once more, apologizing with his eyes. Before he turns away to deal with the situation, I squeeze his hand with mine to show him I understand. And I do because I get it.

I think that's what's necessary to a good relationship. You both have to get where each other are coming from, and understand sometimes it's just not all about you and what you want. Miranda couldn't give him that, but I can, and it's clear he sees it in my eyes because he wraps his arms around me and lowers his lips to mine.

Giving me a hot, blazing kiss, he steals my breath before pulling away and saying against my mouth, "Just so you know, I think you're absolutely wonderful, Caroline. I love you."

I don't even get the chance to respond before he lowers me back to the ground and tosses me a wink before walking away as I try to convince myself he didn't just say what I think he did.

But I don't get to think about it much at all before Frank is ushering me outside to Benedict's car and sending me on my way.

However, it's the only thing on my mind the whole way to his house.

I tried to stay up and wait for him, but the next time I see Benedict is when I wake up at seven a.m. to his arm thrown around my waist, and my body snuggled into his as he sleeps behind me. It's so warm underneath the blankets with him I don't want to get up, and part of me wishes he would wake up so we could have sex, but he isn't. And since I'm pretty sure he hasn't been asleep longer than four hours because of when the club closes, I slip out of bed as gently as I can without waking him, and head downstairs to make something to eat.

Three hours later, after I've eaten, showered, and watched a little t.v. my phone rings, and seeing Nathan's name on the screen, I answer with a smile on my face which I know he can hear as well. "Hey!"

"Hey baby. So good to hear your voice."

"Yeah, I missed yours too. How's it going?"

"God, it's a pain in my ass, but I'm pretty sure I'll be home on New Year's at some point. I can't wait to see you, baby."

He sounds so tired, but more like the man I love, and some of the anxiety that's been squeezing my chest eases as I say softly, "Me too. I don't ever want to experience being apart like this again."

"It sucks, that's for sure, but can't promise I won't have to do this more in the future." He clears his throat. "I'm so glad you're not angry at me, baby. I didn't mean to ignore you, but this is truly my first moment to myself other than when I had to go to bed. I just wanted to make sure I got enough rest to deal with all this bullshit."

"I was a little mad, but only because this is new for both of us, and I felt like you weren't talking to me much. But this was new for both of us and I know you weren't ignoring me on purpose." And I did. Nathan just isn't that type of person; he's always been upfront and honest with me, and I feel silly for letting my imagination run wild. "I'm a little sad you won't be here for New Year's Eve either, but I'm a big girl. I'll get over it."

"Same, baby, but I'm sure you'll have a great New Year's all the same. How're you doing? Anything exciting going on?"

"Not really with me. Just been spending time

with Benedict and Ethan since school's on break. Not much to do really."

"Good, good. You sound much happier than last time, so Benedict must be treating you right. Well, he better be."

With a laugh of happiness, I say, "Yeah, he is. He's great; we're great. I'm looking forward to seeing you though. I'm gonna need some quality alone time with you."

"Looking forward to it, too." He pauses and then sighs, our conversation over as he says, "Well, I'm out of time baby. Time to get back to work. I'll make sure to let you know as soon as I can when I'll be home. Love you."

"Kay. Love you too."

I relax on the couch as the call disconnects, feeling better now that I've gotten to speak to Nathan for more than just a brief moment. All the anxiety and worries over the last few days disappears, and I decide to call Ethan since I know he's been worried about me the last couple of days.

"Caro, something wrong?" Ethan sounds breathless — and worried — as he answers the phone.

"Nah. Nathan just called me and everything's fine. Guess I got all worked up for nothing."

"Oh. Well, awesome. You sound better, too. But

hey, did you hear what happened at the club last night?"

I know he can't see me roll my eyes, but I do it anyway because he had to know I spent most of my time there now. Sometimes I think all the time he spends with Destiny and all the sex they have is rotting his brain. "Yeah, of course. I mean, Benedict just told me he caught two guys. He sent me home though so he could deal with it without worrying about me while I waited for him."

"Right, right. Well, I saw on the news they suspect the guy who was selling it works for the people they've been trying to catch for a while now. I didn't know much about it but guess it's been going on for a few years. I know it's probably not that crazy in a college town that someone's dealing drugs, but kinda odd we didn't hear about it before now, don'tcha think?"

"I dunno. Can't say I've ever thought about it since I've never been interested in drugs."

"Hmm, well make sure you stay safe and keep an eye out. I bet Benedict's pissed they brought it into his club and thought they'd get away with it."

"Yeah, he's not awake yet since he had to deal with the police and all, but I'll probably go wake him up soon since I'm bored." I yawn as he laughs, and then ask him, "What are you up to anyway?"

"Oh, I'm with Destiny. I'm about to go get stuff for the party tomorrow night. You're coming right?"

"Of course! I wouldn't miss it for anything. Nathan told me he probably won't be back 'till New Years during the day at some point, so I'm free. I'll see if Benedict wants to come."

"When doesn't he?"

"Ha, shut up perv. Pretty sure you're the same with Destiny. Put her on the phone so I can ask."

"She's tied up right now. Which means I gotta go, she's probably getting cold."

"Oh my god, Ethan!"

"What? You know I'll always answer your calls no matter what I'm doing, but guess I should go finish so she can come with me." He laughs and I hear Destiny cracking up in the background which makes it clear they are both fucking with me. "Love ya, Caro. See ya."

"Love ya, too."

"All that love going around is making me jealous." Benedict's unexpected and amused remark makes me jump as I hang up the phone, but with a quick recovery, I smile at him as he takes a seat beside me. Putting his arm around my shoulder, I lean into his side after he gives me a short, soft, and sweet kiss. "Morning."

"Hi."

"You must be having a good day since you're grinning like a fool."

Leaning forward, I set the phone on the table and move until I'm straddling Benedict's lap with my arms around his neck. "Yeah, I'm great. Nathan and I finally talked. He misses me as much as I miss him."

"Good. I didn't like seeing you doing nothing but worry." He reciprocates my embrace by putting one arm around my waist and the other on the center of my back, dragging my upper body forward until my t-shirt covered chest is touching his bare one. "Mm, I like you in this position, where I can see down your shirt and feel how hot you are for me as you rub your body against mine."

"Maybe I'm making myself hot." He relocates his hands to my hips, pushing down as he moves his hips, grinding his hard and ready to go cock against me as he demonstrates his desires. Gasping, I wiggle and return the favor, teasing him as much as he's teasing me, saying, "Don't you hate that I'm wearing pajama pants right now? I do. There's something to be said for always having a skirt on because this is fucking inconvenient."

One of his hands leaves my hips and slips under my shirt, cupping and massaging my breast while he grinds against me again, using two fingers to pinch the nipple to make it perk up. He chuckles at my gasp, grinding against me once more before capturing my lips with his, and in what can only be described as one hot, swift, and sexy move, he adjusts position until I'm lying flat on my back on the couch with him between my legs. Our tongues continue to tangle as he uses both hands to pull off my pants, spread my legs, and thrusts into me, making us both moan as he pauses once he's as deep as he can go.

Gripping my hip with one hand again as I wrap my legs around him, I feel his other hand move behind my head and grab a fistful of hair. Dragging his mouth away, I whimper as he tugs on my hair until my neck is exposed, followed up with him kissing down my jaw before heading back toward my ear. He nips at the lobe as he pulls his cock to the tip, pauses, and then plunges back in, making my back bow with the force of it and my eyes flutter shut. For a split second, I actually worry he's going to break the couch from the force of it, and then he laughs softly into my ear.

"I don't know what it is, Caroline, but I just realized we do a lot of fucking on couches."

"We," I say with a lick of my lips, enjoying the feel of him surrounding me but wishing he was still kissing me. "We do a lot of fucking in general. I didn't notice a particular interest in couches."

"No? Perhaps now you will since I've pointed it

out." He moves again, thrusting hard enough the couch moves a little beneath us, and he full on laughs as I squeak in surprise. "Don't worry, this couch is sturdy as hell, or at least it better be considering what I paid for it."

"Oh god."

"Don't worry if it isn't. I'll just buy a new one and we can break that one too."

Now I laugh as he starts kissing down my jaw and back to my lips, brushing them against mine in a soft tease as if he wants me to look at him, but I don't since I'm pretty sure my face is flushed. "Isn't it awkward to fuck me like this with one leg on the ground and the other squished against the back?"

"Not really. I'm rather focused on the feel of your pussy around my cock and the noises you make while we fuck." My eyes pop open at that only to see him gazing down at me with a naughty glint in his. "There you are, beautiful. Now keep them open."

"And if I don't?"

His lips twitch with amusement. "Then I'll quit fucking you, and that wouldn't be nice for either of us, would it?"

"I can't help if you fuck me so hard my eyes can't stay open from the pure pleasure. Now shut up and fuck me like you mean it."

"Ooh, bossy." He tests me by thrusting hard

and fast a few times, and when I keep my eyes locked on his the whole time — just fucking barely! — he leans down as he pauses again to kiss my lips and murmurs against them, "I thought about you all night last night. How you were in my bed, naked and waiting for me, and I couldn't be with you. I've liked having you all to myself, and I'm going to fucking miss you sleeping with me every night."

His statement has me sucking in a breath. "Benedict—"

"I know." He shuts me up with the thrust of his cock and of his tongue, kissing me deep while fucking me hard, and continues talking once I'm gasping for air while he speaks as if he isn't exerting himself at all. "I know you're more complicated than me, but I meant what I said last night. It's all I could think about and honestly, I enjoyed the look of absolute fucking surprise on your face when I told you I love you."

"We haven't known each other very long," I finally manage to say, feeling as if I want to cry but not knowing why. "I didn't expect you to say it so soon."

"Since when does length of time have any control over the way someone feels?" He smiles as I feel my face flush and his gentle kiss makes a tear leak from my eye. "I know how I feel, and I fucking love you Caroline. Whether you feel the same or you're on the way to feeling the same, you tell me when you want to, not when you think you should."

I'm so beyond words at this point, surrounded by this man in every way possible, that I simply give him a nod as he gazes down at me. And he makes it clear he understands how tumultuous my feelings are by giving me a wicked grin and saying, "Now, I'll fuck you like I mean it."

And he does.

"Two minutes until midnight! You ready, Caro?"

Held close in Benedict's arms in his club, which is packed as it is every New Year's Eve, I give Ethan a happy smile. "Hell yeah. I think this is the best party yet!"

"Of course it is, I'm here!"

Destiny and Ethan cling to one another, and the looks on their faces make me so happy for them. You can tell they are in love, and I guess Benedict sees what I do because he puts his mouth real close to my ear and says, "You're welcome."

I know he's saying that because he introduced them, and for a split second, I wonder if it's hard for him to see them together like that since she's Len's sister, but then shove the thought aside. We've seen Len and Miranda a few times since then, and each time it's gotten a little easier, a little less awkward as they seem so genuinely happy.

They came to the party tonight, and while Benedict had hugged Miranda earlier, wishing her a happy new year, Len had only gotten a nod in greeting and not much else. Once they walked away, Benedict explained that Miranda and all her issues meant he blamed Len more for keeping the secrets because it wasn't something he expected of him, and I got it. It was harder for him to forgive Len than it was to forgive Miranda because Len had never betrayed him before. I imagine it would work the same way with Nathan, especially if I were the one to betray him and not Rissa. And that thought is when I notice something.

"Benedict, have you seen Rissa lately?"

He furrows his brow as he gazes down at me, probably wondering why I am suddenly asking him such a random question, and then shakes his head along with a shrug. "No. I figured she went home for the holidays."

"Oh. Yeah, I guess that would make sense since she's not from around here."

"I'm glad you live here." He moves so my back is against the bar and he's got me trapped with no way to escape. Not that I would want to anyway. "I don't think I would like you being gone for weeks, leaving me with nothing but my hand for company."

"Hey, even your hand needs a little love every now and then. I'm sure it's feeling rejected lately, you focusing your attention on me and all. Give it a little love already!"

As his lips curve, his eyes light up, and his lips move dangerously close to mine, he grabs one of my hands with his and slides it down the side of my body before moving them in between both of ours. He uses his hand to press my palm against the bulge in his pants, holding it in place as he gives tiny thrusts of his hips to encourage me to play, and that's when the countdown starts as everyone in the room starts yelling.

"Ten!"

Benedict moves his hips to trap my hand there and uses both of his hands to hold my head still, our lips barely a breath from melding, and says, "Tell me Caroline."

"Nine!"

"Tell you what?"

"Eight!"

"I see it in your eyes sweetheart," he growls, using his teeth to give a gentle bite to my bottom lip. "You look at me like Ethan looks at Destiny, so say it."

"Seven!"

"Benedict—" I don't know how I look at him, but I do know how I feel. I've been falling in love with him from the moment we've met and if anything, the way he makes me feel only gets stronger every day we spend together. And I want to tell him, but the words just stick in my throat and I'm not sure I should say them. Because once I do, there's no going backward; there's no letting him go no matter what.

"Six!"

He drops one of his hands, causing my eyes to widen as I feel him grip the bottom of my skirt and yanking it up until I'm close to being bared, even though the fact we're surrounded by people and closed in means nobody knows what's going on except the two of us. I spread my legs a little to give him better access, closing my eyes with delicious anticipation.

The thrust of two of his fingers into my pussy while his thumb stimulates my clit is simultaneous with the room as it yells the next number in unison. "Five!"

"A kiss and an orgasm at midnight, Caroline. Who d'ya love?"

"Four!"

"Oh...you—you play dirty." I can't drop my head back because he's holding it in place, and he chuckles against my lips as I gasp because he's touching and stroking me just right, winding my body tighter and tighter to the point I know I can't fight it. He's going to get me off right here at the bar in his club and I don't care. I don't want him to stop. I want him as much as he wants me, all the time. "Fuck."

"Three!"

"Yes, I do. And I'll fuck you later, Caroline, promise."

"Two!"

"Benedict?" I feel him smile against my mouth at my high pitched voice as my body hovers on the edge of orgasm, and as it starts to roll over me I give him what he wants and what I want too as I say against his mouth, "I love you."

"One!"

Time doesn't matter anymore as I come around his fingers and he covers my lips the moment I make a sound, which is a split second before the room erupts into yells of 'Happy New Year!' but we aren't paying attention. I'm wrapped around Benedict, the pleasure he's given me in one of the most perfect moments of my life shooting through me, and he's kissing me like he's the happiest man in the world while he removes his fingers from inside me and puts my skirt back into place.

When we finally stop kissing, I let him know what I think of his tactics by taking his bottom lip between my teeth and nipping it. Of course, he doesn't care as he laughs softly and slips a hand to my ass before giving it a pinch, which makes me object just like he knew it would and I let go of his lip to object. "Hey!"

"Hey." The smile on his face is wide and happy, his eyes warm and filled with tenderness as he pushes my hair behind my ear before saying with a wink, "I love you too, Caroline. Here's to a wonderful new year."

"Yeah!" Ethan jumps into the convo, stepping close to kiss me on the cheek. "Happy New Year, Caro. Sounds like you're off to a good start."

"I am."

"Me, too." Destiny comes up beside him and he wraps his arm around her waist, then tosses me a grin. "Guess what?"

"What?"

Destiny holds up her hand, but it takes me a moment to register it's her left hand, and she's showing me a ring.

A ring.

And it takes Benedict saying, "Wow, congratulations you two," before I register Ethan is engaged to Destiny, and he's standing there grinning at me, waiting for a response.

I open my mouth and then shut it, realizing that saying I love you is nothing compared to

Ethan proposing to Destiny, whom he met after I met Benedict. I'm so shocked by this I'm not even sure what to say to Ethan. I mean, he didn't even tell me he was going to propose or anything, and I wonder why the hell not. We usually tell each other everything, especially something like this, and even if it doesn't make sense really, I'm hurt at not knowing he was planning to do such a thing.

But now is not the time or place, so I force a smile to my face and step forward to hug him before he guesses something is wrong. "Congratulations, guys! This is such a surprise!"

"Well," Ethan says into my ear, hugging me back. "When you know, you know, right?"

"Definitely. I can't believe it though!"

"Me either!" Destiny leans in to give me a hug when I let go of Ethan and I pat her back awkwardly. "He completely shocked me but oh god, I can't wait!"

Lucky for me, my phone buzzes on the counter behind me, which I pick up once she lets me go.

"Oh, it's Nathan! I've gotta take this."

"You can use my office Caroline." Benedict steps out of my way and gives me a quick peck on the lips. "I'll wait for you here."

I acknowledge him with a smile even as I put a finger in one ear to block out the noise while I answer the phone with my other hand, lifting it up to my ear as I walk toward his office.

"Happy New Year, baby," he says the moment he realizes I've picked up. "You at the club?"

"Yeah, I am. Wish you were here."

"Actually," he says with a laugh. "I am. I'm standing near the front entrance, inside the door. I'm super tired and want to go home to sleep, but come and give me a hug real quick?"

With a squeal of happiness, I hang up the phone and turn around, looking for the quickest path to the front of the club. Finding it, I take off at a run, squeezing past anyone and everyone I can until I do exactly that. One of the bouncers nods at me as I walk out of the second entryway and that's when I see Nathan standing right inside the main door. The blatant look of relief he gets confuses me, but then he opens his arms and I walk right into them.

Enveloping me in his arms, our lips find one another with ease, and he smiles down at me when he pulls back a second later. "Hey. So fucking happy to see you, baby."

His exhaustion practically pours from him, noticeable even in his voice, and his eyes have dark circles around them, but he still looks thrilled to see me. And I'm equally as excited to see him.

"Let me go get my coat. We can go home together."

With a shake of his head, he gives me another quick kiss before dropping his arms from around me. "I'm just gonna go home and pass out, baby. That's why I came here so we could see each other. I was just gonna go home but I didn't want you to find me there in the morning and get upset I didn't tell you I was back. So, stay here and have fun with everyone, for me, okay?"

I wish I could say I understand, but I don't. I'd lie next to him even if I'm wide awake if it meant I would be close to him. But — and I don't know what it is — something tells me he wants me to do as he asks and not take it personally. He's tired, he looks it, and he just wants to go to sleep. I try to turn my frown back into a smile, but it's hard because I just want to go home with him.

As always, he knows what's going on in my head, lifting a hand to stroke my cheek as he gives me another soft smile. "I love you. We'll spend the whole day together tomorrow, and it'll be way better than right now when I'm so exhausted I can barely see straight, all right?"

"Yeah." I nod, trying to convince myself more than him that I'm okay with this. "Yeah. I love you, too."

"Caroline, what the—" Benedict's voice from

behind me has both me and Nathan jumping. Whirling to face him, his eyes widen when he recognizes exactly who I'm talking to. "Oh, hey man. I wondered why she took off running like a crazy person. Sorry. Didn't mean to interrupt."

"Nah, it's okay. I'm going home to pass out anyway. See you in the morning baby." Nathan brushes his lips against mine, then looks over at Benedict as he says, "Take care of her man."

"Always."

With a final lingering glance at me, Nathan turns and walks out the door into the night, leaving me there staring at his back as tears fill my eyes.

"I don't understand," I whisper as Benedict steps close and pulls me close to his side. "He didn't want to me to go home with him. Said he just wants to sleep and I should stay here and have fun."

"He looked pretty tired, sweetheart. He probably didn't want to put an end to your night just so you could go home and watch him sleep."

I wish it were that simple, but something about this whole thing bugs me, as it has since he took his trip in the first place. And even though he left me here, now all I'll think about is how he's at home and I'm not with him.

Something I'm pretty sure Benedict realizes because he sighs and says, "If you're that worried, let me make sure the staff can take care of things here and I'll take you home."

"Thank you."

It's not even thirty minutes later when we leave the club to take me home, Benedict holding my hand the whole way.

CHAPTER TWENTY-FOUR

When we get to the house, Benedict insists on walking me up to the door, and even though it's not a far walk from the driveway, it is pitch black out. I'm not really sure why Nathan hadn't turned on the porch light like he always does, but I suppose that's the least of my concerns right now.

It's real quiet as I enter after unlocking the door with Benedict right behind me, and when his body tenses against mine, his fingers tightening on my shoulders, I'm instantly on alert.

"What?"

"Shh. Do you hear that?"

After listening for a few seconds, I whisper, "No. I don't hear anything. Are you trying to scare me?"

"Of course not. Maybe it's just the tv."

"Probably. He likes to watch it to go to sleep." Shrugging out of my coat with a roll of my eyes, I hang up my coat in the closet while Benedict shuts the door softly behind him. When I finish doing that, I turn to face him with my hands on my hips and raise a brow. "Planning to spend the night?"

"Course not. You want to be alone with Nathan and I completely understand. I will miss you though." He steps real close and backs me up against the wall, planting his hands palm down while lowering his head toward mine. "Give me a kiss goodbye."

Slipping my hands inside his jacket, I slide my hands up his chest slowly, locking his hot gaze with my own naughty one accompanied by an equally wicked grin. Then, lifting one hand to each side of his face so each cups a cheek, I move in enough to press our lips together, and he's instantly taking advantage of our position.

Not wanting to deny myself or him the pleasure we feel when we're touching each other, my mouth opens under the pressure from his, and his tongue invades my mouth like I'm sure he wants to invade my pussy with his cock. His body presses into mine and a small jerk of his hips has mine hitting the door, but that isn't what makes me still and push on Benedict's shoulder.

It's the shout of a woman's voice I don't recognize coming from upstairs.

Benedict pushes off without a word and ducking under his arm, I take off down the hall until I reach the stairs and pause as Nathan replies, his words muffled.

"Stop," Benedict whispers as he comes up beside me. "Let's try to hear what they're saying before you run up there."

I'm angry at the idea Nathan lied to me, but more confused at why he'd find it necessary. "If he wanted to be alone with someone, why didn't he just say so? Why tell me he was going to bed?"

"I dunno," he hisses, snatching my hand with his while using his other to grip my jaw and make me look at him. "Calm down. I didn't see a car other than his and yours outside. Maybe somebody showed up?"

I rip my hand from his to throw my arms up in the air in a frustrated gesture. "At nearly one a.m.? Who just shows up unannounced that late unless—"

A loud crash from Nathan's bedroom makes us both jump, and we both stare at each other wide-eyed. I'm the first to react, taking the steps two at a time while Benedict trails behind me, and once we're both at the top of the steps, we walk as quietly as possible toward the bedroom. I'm glad for the soft carpet beneath my feet making it so no footsteps can be heard but it doesn't help the roiling of my stomach as we inch closer.

Benedict pulls out his phone and swipes across the screen until the dialer pops up. We're halfway down the hall when I stop because the woman's voice starts up again, and it's clear I don't know this woman, but I listen as they fight back and forth because I have no idea what's going on in the slightest.

"Why are you mad at me? You're the lying sack of fucking shit here!"

"I didn't lie! How many times do I have to tell you that?"

"No? What the hell are you doing living in this house? With that woman?"

"I told you, Rox—"

"I don't fucking care for your excuses! Start explaining yourself now, or I'll shoot you. I fucking swear I will!"

"Baby, please, you know it's complicated—"

His term of endearment for me, directed at her, rips into my heart. Even in all the time he dated Rissa, I've never heard him call anyone baby except me.

Yet it's clear the woman doesn't care what he calls her. She's getting more hysterical by the moment as her voice continues to rise, and I wonder who she is, whether she really has a gun aimed at Nathan, and how they are connected. "No it's not, not fucking complicated at all. I followed you here from the airport because I knew you were full of bullshit. You're just pissed I found you; I told you I would, didn't I? And so did my daddy. How dare you fucking leave me behind without even saying goodbye!"

Benedict touches my arm and when I look up at him, he puts a finger to his mouth to indicate I should stay quiet and lifts his phone in the air. Taking a step back and then another, he disappears until I can barely see him around the corner and I realize he's calling the police.

For a brief moment I consider if I should just leave. It's obvious Nathan hadn't wanted me here, and maybe this is why. Maybe he knew this crazy person was going to show up and he hadn't wanted me around it. But now I'm worried about him. How does he know her? Why did she say he left her behind? If she followed him from the airport, had she seen him with me? It's clear she knows about me and Rissa so he must've told her? And most of all, if he's in trouble and has been, why wouldn't he tell me?

Hearing the faintest sound of Benedict talking into the phone, I step closer to the door to listen once more to their arguing, more confused than I've ever been. But it's not long before she answers at least one of my questions.

"You said you were working, trying to keep us safe, but you were here, fucking two other women! How can you think I'll ever trust you again?" He mutters something I can't hear and she laughs with clear disbelief. "You've been gone four fucking years and when you finally come home it's to tell me you want a divorce! After all we've been through? After all I've done for you..."

I don't know what she says after that because I back away from the door, horror at realizing Nathan's lied to me all this time spreading through my whole body. Questions fly through my mind so fast I'm not even sure what I'm thinking and they mix with the feelings of betrayal and confusion and anger. I don't understand what I just heard, it doesn't mesh with the life I've had with Nathan, with our relationship.

Two minutes. Five. In reality, I don't know how much time passes, but when the sound of sirens finally registers in my ears, the question of whether or not she actually has a gun is answered.

One shot is fired, followed quickly by another.

My mouth drops open, but I don't know whether I scream or not, my whole world in a blur as I fall to my knees. Did she shoot him? Was she going to come shoot me if she heard me scream? I don't even care. At this point, I wish she would because the pain couldn't possibly be any worse.

And when a third shot is fired a few seconds after the first two, I feel Benedict lift me off the floor and start to carry me away as tears stream down my face. But I don't want to go. I want to see if Nathan is okay and I start kicking my legs, screaming, "Let me go! I have to see if he's okay!"

"Goddamnit, calm down Caroline! The cops are here. Let them come up and make sure it's safe." He keeps walking, keeping me secure even as I stop fighting him, and heads down the steps.

"She shot him. Oh god, she had to have shot him. She said she was his wife."

He finally sets me down after carrying me outside and pulls me against him. "I'm so sorry, sweetheart. You shouldn't've heard that. You don't know if anything she said is true."

"I don't... I don't understand—"

The next little while is hazy as the police arrive, shock taking hold of me and refusing to let go, but when the police come back down and shake their head at both of us, the look on Benedict's face is all I see.

A look that tells me the love of my life is dead, as is the woman who murdered him.

And with that, my entire life changes.

CHAPTER TWENTY-FIVE

"Ready to go back to school?"

My mother's question diverts my attention from the view out the plane window over to her. Giving her a petulant shrug, I return to what I was doing and she sighs in the heavy, worried way I imagine every mother perfects when they have children.

"One semester, darling." She rests a hand on my shoulder after giving it a light pat. "Graduating in December instead of May like you planned, but that's not surprising with all that went on."

"Sure."

She gives up trying to talk to me after that, which is great, because I don't really want to converse with anyone. I wish my father were the one sitting next to me, because he wouldn't try to tell me anything. We're a lot alike in that way; he understood when I said I needed to get away and other than a hug upon seeing me, has left me in relative peace, except for the moments when my mother dragged him in to 'help' get through to me. I wish my mother would do like my father does more often, no matter how much she thinks she's helping me by, frankly, being up my ass for all this time.

I love her, but in my whole life, she's never been this attentive and unsurprisingly, she's smothering me to the point I'm looking forward to not being around her. Terrible considering all I've ever wanted was for my parents to spend time with me, but perhaps by not spending so much time with me when I was younger, it means I can't handle it now as an adult.

Either way, eight and half months has been long enough. I'm ready to go back to not seeing them for six months at a time again.

Once the plane lands, we pick up our luggage, and once outside, get into the waiting car. My father rattles off two addresses, my mother snuggles into my father's side, and I stare out the window as it starts to pour down rain.

A fitting beginning to my return, since I feel like bursting into tears. I don't though. I hold them back as I always do, because crying never does me any favors, and it's not long before we arrive where I'll be living for the semester: Ethan's place.

We all get out and as my father tells the driver which luggage pieces are mine, I turn to stare at the apartment building for a moment while the rain pelts down on my umbrella. Then I pull out my phone and send a text to Ethan asking him to come downstairs. I'm sure my parents would help me take my stuff up, but I'd rather they just get in the car and leave.

As Ethan approaches, the driver finishes getting my luggage and gets back into the car while my parents and I say goodbye.

"Honey." My mother pulls me into a hug, kissing the top of my head before letting me go with a strained smile. "Love you. If you need anything, call me."

"Okay, I will. Love you, too." At this point I think she needs the assurance more than I do, but chances are I won't call her, and we both know it.

My father hauls me into his arms with an exaggerated growl and holds on a little longer than my mother did. Then he lets go after telling me he loves me and to stay strong, and as they both get back into the car, Ethan grabs my attention.

"Come on then, Caro," he says, grabbing the handles of two of my luggage and jerking his water-sopped head toward the building. "Let's get inside before we're soaked."

I grab the third and follow him when my

parent's car finally drives away. Once we're inside the building, and then his first floor apartment, he insists I sit down while he puts my stuff in the room I'll be staying in, so I do.

And the next thing I know, I wake up as Ethan carries me in his arms, registering this fact seconds before he places me gently on the bed. It's dark though and he doesn't see I'm awake as he pulls up the blankets to cover me.

When he starts to rise, I grab his arm and whisper, "Please don't leave me."

"Caro." He lowers his head into his hands and for a moment I think he'll be the one to break down instead of me, but he takes a deep breath and turns back toward me. Slipping under the blankets, he drags me into his embrace, holding me tight as I hide my face in his shoulder. "I would never leave you. I'm so glad you're back."

I don't know what to say. I'm not glad I'm back. I just did it because I need to finish school and transferring isn't an option, not when I'm so close to graduating from this one. I'd have preferred not to end up back here again. Fuck the fact my friends are here, my parents when they were in the country, and that I grew up here. And I want to get it out of the way so I can leave once and for all. I still have no idea what I want to do with my life, but I can figure that out later. Right now, I just want to survive the next sixteen weeks. But there is one thing I can't deny, and that's the words I say.

"I missed you, too."

And for a few minutes, we're both silent, so quiet I think he'll let me get away with it. He won't make me face it, he won't say his name, he won't make me do something I've been avoiding for almost three-fourths of a year. But Ethan...he knows me better than anyone else, and as he holds me tight in his arms so I can't leave, he does the one thing not even my parents or the counselor had the courage to do.

"Nathan wouldn't have wanted this."

The sound of his name makes me tense up, and even though I know from experience with wrestling Ethan all these years that his hold is strong, and I won't get loose no matter how much I fight, I still try. Wriggling in his grasp, a strength I didn't know I had almost gets me free, but then he pins me underneath him and holds my arms above my head.

"Stop it," he hisses, a rough push of his arms on my wrists causing me to go motionless when matched with the banked ire in his voice. "I know he lied to you. I know he wasn't who he said he was; we all know Caro. None of us, *none* of us, have the right to tell you how to feel or how long, but this zombie like state you're in? It's unacceptable. You haven't cried, I know you well enough to know you haven't let it out, and you need to. The pain won't heal even a little if you don't, and you know it."

I can barely see him and I know it's the same for him, but as the emotions I've been ignoring well up in my chest, and the tears try to push to the surface, I turn my head to the side as if not looking in his direction will make him stop speaking. Of course, it doesn't.

"Nothing in the world can make it better, Caro. Nothing will take it back. You can't unmeet him, un-love him, or undo anything that happened. And, while I'm pissed at him for lying to all of us, I do know one thing for sure. He loved you Caro. He did. You can be mad at the type of person he was, the type of person he used to be, the life he was running from, but he didn't fake *that*, Caro. He didn't fake his fucking love for you. He wanted you, Caro. He was going to fucking propose to you."

That finally gets a reaction out of me: a snort of absolute disbelief. Turning my back to him, I glare even though he can't see me and spit out, "So? He was already fucking married! He could've proposed all he wanted, but you can't get married when you already are, even under a different name. At least, not fucking legally. He wasn't on a job at all; he went there to see *her*. Roxanne. You know, his wife?"

"Yeah, Caro," he retorts, his tired voice softening along with his hold, but not enough for me to get free if I tried to. "The wife he hadn't seen in nearly four years or had any contact with for the majority of it. The wife who had an arrest record a mile long as a juvie and belonged to a family of drug dealers. You know, the family he testified against, the family where he got some of them put behind bars?"

"Not her, obviously, or he'd still be breathing."

"And, if he were, would you forgive him for lying to try and protect his ass? And yours?"

Truth is, I don't know. How could I know, when I never got the opportunity to even try?

After his death, I found out who Nathan really was. I don't think he faked his life with me, or his feelings, or anything like that. Yes, it's hard not to question his love for me when he pretty much hid everything about himself except the things he was safe to share, but deep down, I know he loved me. And when the police had shown me evidence about his previous life, the life which had caught up with him, it had been hard to believe.

His name wasn't Nathan MacMillan, which ended up being a made up identity with papers he'd obviously had made for the right price, but

Nicholas Travosky. A man who married Roxanne O'Rourke, his high school sweetheart, at eighteen, and at age twenty, had gone into hiding following his testimony after receiving death threats. His wife — even calling her that in my mind leaves a bad taste in my mouth but that's what she was — had been sixteen when they married with the permission of her parents and her husband had protected her, saying she had nothing to do with any of it, but the police were positive that wasn't true. However, they couldn't prove it, and she'd spent the last four years staying out of any sort of trouble; well, that they knew of.

So, why hadn't he taken her with him when they disappeared? That's what I asked, but they didn't have an answer. There weren't answers for a lot of things I wanted to know, and that meant I would never know. Six months after he left his life as Nicholas and became Nathan, following his apparent promise to his wife that he would come back when it was safe, is when he met me.

And for nearly four years, he'd simply been Nathan, the man with a simple job, and a relatively uncomplicated life.

Until Roxanne found him with the help of a few family members who then turned around and began a drug dealing operation right here in the town where Nathan lived. Police showed me all the records from Nathan's phone, where she'd finally contacted him and threatened to expand her little business unless he returned home to her, where he managed to get a promise out of her that if he came home she would get the drugs out of here, and the message she sent after he'd come back following his declaration about divorcing her. A message which said she would kill him as soon as she got the chance because she was the only person in this relationship who was allowed to end it.

Turns out he received that message minutes before he came into the club to see me on New Years.

Everything I heard before those shots though... a lot of what she said still didn't make sense. But it's clear Roxanne had been insane and all evidence pointed toward Nathan trying to end things with her once and for all before that night. He knew though; he knew she would never let him go, and that's why he insisted I stay at the club and enjoy myself. It's why he'd looked straight at Benedict and told him to take care of me.

Because he'd meant it literally.

"Caro? Where did you go?"

Ethan snaps his fingers in my face to get my attention, making me jerk a little in his arms, but that's all it takes for all my pent up emotions to fight their way out.

Because truth is, I'm mad at a man who wanted to keep me out of harm's way, who died at the hands of the one person who refused to let him go. A man who came to see me at the club, who planned to take me home with him after a long week apart, yet apparently had made a decision seconds before I flew into his arms to leave me behind.

The cops said based on the timeline they put together, she arrived at the house only fifteen minutes before Benedict and I had, and that was information they got from the taxi service she'd taken to the house. They thought Nathan had been packing when she showed up, planning to leave because of her threat, and had continued to pack as they argued. They also said there's no way to know why she chose to shoot him and then herself considering it appeared she was getting what she wanted — him returning home, to her.

All details everybody knew now, including me, and until this point, I kept telling myself it didn't matter. He lied to me, he kept me in the dark, and in my opinion, put us all in danger. But he did try to diffuse the situation, he did try to get her far away from here, from me and Rissa, and he was going to give us up to make that happen because she'd made it clear she wouldn't stop.

He loved me and tried to protect me to the very end.

And he'd paid for it with his life.

"You're wrong," I finally whisper to Ethan as tears begin trickling down my cheeks. "I don't want to have not met him, or not loved him. I just wish it would've had a different ending."

He says nothing because there's nothing he can say and we both know it. He takes me with him and gathers me into his arms once he's on his back, holding me tight as I finally do something I should've done all those months ago.

I let my broken heart grieve like it's never grieved before as I break down, sobbing so hard I can't breathe, in the arms of my best friend who joins me in my despair with tears of his own.

CHAPTER TWENTY-SIX

Two days later, it's the first day of classes.

Ethan and I are in the kitchen as Destiny, at her own insistence, makes breakfast for all of us. As she's flitted around, grabbing this and that, it seems as if it's nearly impossible for her and Ethan not to touch for more than a minute. A shoulder pat here, a peck on the lips there, and after a few of those, I lowered my eyes and have kept them on my phone, which rests on the table where we sit.

I'm so happy for them, I really am, but I can't handle seeing their affection right now.

And when I finally pay attention, Destiny's put the food down in front of me, and is sitting next to Ethan. The two of them talk low, with only eyes for each other, and it makes my heart hurt.

"I'm gonna go eat in my room guys," I say while

rising from my seat. "Got an hour anyway, should make sure I'm ready to go."

They both jerk their gaze away from one another and look at me, equivalent frowns on their face.

Ethan is the first to speak. "Do you want to drive yourself or are you going with us?"

"Neither. I'll probably walk."

"What? You can't—"

Putting up a hand to halt him, I use my free hand to grab my phone and toss him a smirk. "I'm kidding. I'll drive there on my own. Thanks though."

Before either of them can say anything else, or bring up topics I have no desire to discuss in an effort to make me stay here, me and my food exit the kitchen to go upstairs. Once I'm in my room, I shut the door behind me, locking it for good measure.

Then, sitting at my computer, I set my phone down and do the one thing I haven't done the whole time I've been gone: check my email.

And discover pages worth of emails from Benedict interspersed with emails from everywhere else.

Heart thumping in my chest, my eyes stayed glued to the screen as I eat my breakfast, debating in my head whether I want to read the emails now or later, after classes are over for the day.

I've no idea what they will say.

I hadn't even gotten the chance to get used to the idea I'd fallen in love with Benedict before Nathan died. Less than two hours separated the time between my declaration at the club and the fatal shot.

And since a few hours after the cops took our statements, I haven't seen him at all.

All my choice. I haven't even known if we were still together or not, but I'm guessing by the sheer volume of emails he sent me, the answer is yes we are.

Either that or he's cussed me out a lot all this time, thinking I was ignoring him, which since in a way I was, okay. Setting the plate down off to the side, I mentally prepare to handle the worst, but try to expect the best.

I lift my left hand to where the necklace from Benedict used to be while using my right to click on the first email, the one dated the day after Nathan died.

It has three simple words: *I'm sorry, Caroline.*

Tears blur my sight as I click through to the next one: *I love you.*

And the next: *I'm here for you.*

On and on with simple yet supportive

statements, until I reach the one where I left town a week after Nathan's funeral: *I wish you had stayed with me, but I understand why you left. I look forward to seeing you again.*

The strength of the emotion pushing against my eyes, begging for release, makes it impossible to continue. Exiting out of my email, I make my way over to the bed, curling up in a ball in the center of it while giving into the tears I don't have the strength to keep inside any longer.

Crying won't solve anything, but I did feel better after the other night with Ethan. I hate crying though. It makes my head and eyes ache along with the way it feels like my heart clenches real tight in my chest as I sob, as if it's being squeezed to the point of bursting. In the past, I often thought there were moments when I should cry, and I would try, but I didn't. And that's when I realized the kind of emotional distance I had which others didn't seem, well, gifted with. I liked, and still like, the fact a lot of things don't have the ability to upset me.

I thought the same thing would happen with Nathan, but I think most of my inability to cry over it in all the time I've been gone is because I put so much distance between me and our life here together, I didn't have to think about it. I ignored it and I know that's why I finally broke; I have no shield anymore. My life is right in front of my face and I can't ignore it.

Just like I can't ignore Benedict anymore, not that he deserves it. But, there's one fact I can't disregard: he will forever remind me of my life with Nathan. It's simply inevitable, and I don't know how to handle that. One big reason I haven't spoken to him is that I don't know how to proceed; I no longer know how he fits into my life, because my whole life is different now, whether I like it or not.

Rolling onto my back, I use the back of my hands to swipe the tears on my cheeks away even as new ones fall, and try to focus on something else as I take deep breaths in and letting them out slowly.

My phone buzzes to tell me someone sent me a text, and then it's followed up by my alarm going off telling me it's time to head to class.

I seriously debate whether I want to go or not for a moment, but this is exactly why I'm back here. So, with a final swipe at my face to wipe away any leftover emotions, I climb out of bed and walk over to my desk.

Picking up my phone and swiping across the screen, a text from Benedict pops up: *I'm so glad you're back, Caroline. I miss you.*

I'm not sure how he knows I'm back unless Ethan or Destiny told him; I'm going to guess it was Destiny.

Slipping the phone into my backpack without responding, I head downstairs and after locking up — Ethan and Destiny must've left without me hearing them — I get into my car and head toward the school.

It's weird how having been gone so long makes everything look so different when it's not in reality. It's early enough the roads aren't super busy and when I see my favorite cafe, I decide to stop for a latte.

I should've known he would be here, as the delicious scent of the cologne he wears that I love reaches my nose seconds before his arms wrap around me from behind as I stand in line, and he rests his chin on the top of my head.

"Hey," he says softly, sighing when he realizes I'm not going to pull away, and his hold tightens a fraction.

"Hey."

"Headed to class?"

"Yeah."

We take a step forward as the line moves, and with a light chuckle he asks, "Are you going to look at me?"

Oh, I wish I could, but give him a shake of my head. "No. I—I can't. I need to keep it together right now. For class."

"All right." I hear the sadness mixed with

humor in his voice and it almost makes me smile. Almost. "Well, you know you're welcome to break down in my arms any time Caroline. I'll hold you for as long as you'll let me."

"I know."

After we take two more steps forward and I say nothing else, he kisses the top of my head before moving his mouth to my ear to whisper, "Love you. I'll see you later today."

Something in his voice has me thinking it sounded more like a promise than a statement of hope as he releases me, and curiosity has me turning around to tell him I'm not ready to talk, but all I see is the back of him as he exits the cafe.

But I don't have to think about it long.

Turns out, when I walk into my second class of the day, he's standing at the front of the room.

And if I were the type of person who believed in souls and people's eyes able to burn you, his would be searing his initials right into my heart as he stares at me. I just know it.

Until he rips his eyes away and doesn't look at me again, leaving me feeling all alone in a room full of people.

"I HAD two whole classes today and he had to pick mine."

Destiny and Ethan exchange amused glances mixed with exasperation as I plop into a chair in the living room with a sigh, having just returned from school and filling them in on my first day at their request.

"I doubt he did it on purpose," Ethan says.

"No, of course not. But picking me for an internship in his club? That was on fucking purpose."

"I'm sure it was. You know he's a great boss and a terrific role model. You will learn lots about managing a business. I'm not seeing the problem."

"Uh, you mean besides the obvious?"

"Okay, and? Maybe you could do with a little play. Sex is a natural anti-depressant."

"And an anti-histamine," Destiny tosses in, until I glare at her and she turns away with a smirk.

"I have to go see him tonight. He made it very clear we had the *last* appointment."

"Well, we know what he has planned, don't we?" Ethan and Destiny laugh together while I roll my eyes at their immaturity.

"Seriously guys."

"Sorry Caro, but I'm with him. He misses you, and now you'll get to spend lots of time together.

Unless you want to talk to your teacher into switching you..."

I sigh and shake my head. "He said the teams were final. New guy. Probably had no idea Benedict and I know each other. Or...you know, about Nathan and everything."

"Bummer. You could always drop it."

"Don't be ridiculous," I scoff, laughing a little at the conversation and myself. "I don't want to avoid him that badly. I love him, I'm just...I wanted to be ready on my own."

Ethan walks over to the chair and leans down to hug me. "We know. So, tell him that and understand it's probably just as difficult for him. One moment you were there, the next you were gone for eight months with no word."

"I know." My words are muffled in his shoulder.

And I do. I'm not ignoring everybody else's grief, because I know Nathan's death affected more people than me alone. I'm just having trouble with my own. Something I'm sure everybody who loves me knows, people who want to comfort me as much as they want support, and which makes me feel guilty for struggling as I am to let anyone in.

Something made even harder by the fact I know my reaction would probably disappoint Nathan a bit. He talked to me many times about how having more than one relationship was more than about love and sex. It also brought support; more people to be there when shit hit the fan for you. He may not have known he was going to die, but that's why he told Benedict to take care of me. He knew he loved me and he would, but he probably hadn't counted on me pulling away like I had. Or maybe he had, since he knew me pretty well.

I don't know. I'll never know, and that's it for me. I'll never see him in the flesh again. All I have are memories and pictures and that's it. He's gone and at times, I wish I was too because I miss him so much.

I hear rather than see Destiny leave the room, and Ethan lets me go, only to sit on the arm of the chair while tossing his arm across my shoulders. Leaning to the side, his head rests lightly on mine as he says, "We hung out, you know. Me and him. A lot."

"You did?"

"Yeah." He laughed, although it was a bit sad sounding. "Between you being gone, and Miranda and Len getting married, and them having their baby...he was a mess."

Oh, shit. I forgot all about them and their baby. And Benedict, left here without me after Miranda leaving him.

Suddenly I'm angry at myself, and wondering if he wrote me about this stuff in the rest of the emails I still haven't checked, and now I'm not sure I want to. I've no doubt I've caused him pain on top of everything else, because I felt it this morning in the cafe as he held me.

And as I refused to turn around and look at him.

But I saw him, all right. I saw him in class earlier, looking as if he hadn't slept, his clothes a little disheveled as if he hadn't been taking care of himself, yet tried to make sure he was presentable enough to come to the school. Where, other than a brief yet felt-like-forever glance, he hadn't looked at me again. Not even before he left.

Sitting here, as every minute passes by, I'm becoming more sure his plans for later involve making me pay for how things have been, and how it's clear they still are.

"I should probably get going," I finally say, looking at the glaring clock to see my appointment with Benedict is in a half hour. "He'll be waiting for me."

"Okay." With a final squeeze of my shoulders, Ethan lets go with a final, soft comment. "Be gentle, Caroline. He may be a man — you know, how everybody thinks guys should be so tough, not cry — but he's just as breakable as you. As anyone."

That brings a small smile to my face as I stand. "I don't think you're less of a man 'cuz you cried with me, Ethan."

"I know you don't. And it's because you're not a bitch, even if you come across like one sometimes."

"Gee, thanks."

"Your cold little heart is welcome," he tosses back with a snicker before turning away. "Love ya, Caro. Later!"

Lifting my middle finger at his retreating back, I say, "Love you too, jackass."

Then, after a few deep breaths, I head out to the club for my meeting with Benedict.

"Ah, Caroline," Frank says with a wide grin from behind the bar. "So glad to see you again."

"You too, Frank." The smile I give back to him is genuine as I walk past him toward Benedict's office. "Is he ready?"

"Yeah. When you're done, you come out here and give me a hug, all right?"

"I will."

"Good."

Nothing more is said as I walk out of his sight and upon seeing the door is standing wide open, I just walk right in.

"Shut the door behind you, Caroline."

He doesn't even look up from his desk as he says this, and with a huff, I ask, "How did you even know it was me?"

"Everybody else knocks even when the door is open, that's how."

"Oh."

"I'm waiting."

Thinking he's not going to look up at me until I shut the door, I pivot on my heel and shut it, making sure to press the lock even though I don't think it's necessary. It became a habit after the one time we had sex in his office and I forgot, although the chance of being caught had given us both quite the thrill, in my opinion.

Facing him once more, I slowly walk toward him while he still doesn't look up at me. But, he does look better than he did this afternoon. He's wearing a different suit, his hair is less unruly, and there is no five o'clock shadow in sight.

"How are you?" His voice rings out firm and clear as he scribbles on something on his desk. "How was the first day of classes?"

"You mean other than having my boyfriend show up in one of mine without warning?"

Jerking his head up at that, he drops the pen as his lips twist — in what way, I'm not sure. All I know is, I get the feeling it isn't good seconds before he makes it clear it's not.

"Are we together, Caroline? Because I'm not quite sure where we stand, to be honest."

I wet my lips with a swipe of my tongue across

my lips, feeling awkward standing in the center of his office, as if the ocean I put between me and him for eight and a half months continues to separate us. And I'm not able to answer his question because I don't know either. I wish I did, but I don't. I suppose since we didn't talk about breaking up, we're still together, but also, nearly three-fourths of a year without speaking to each other might count as breaking up. I can't say for sure because my relationship experience is limited to Nathan and Benedict.

"I'm not really sure," he says while leaning back in his chair and placing both of his hands behind his head, glaring as he continues with, "why you would think you're the only one grieving and leave us all behind as if we're nothing. I only knew you were alive and where you were because you occasionally updated Ethan. Why the hell didn't you tell me as well?"

I give him as honest an answer as I could while tears prick my eyes. "I wasn't thinking about it like that. I...I wasn't thinking at all. Just feeling." And with a struggling breath as I try to hold them at bay, "I was completely out of my depth. I still am."

"And I wasn't?" His laugh is not an amused one. "It's like you didn't give two shits about anything or anyone else except yourself. I feel like a prick for saying that, because you two loved each other so much, but for fucks sake. After the way we both made clear how we felt about each other, for you to just up and leave without a word—"

He cuts off as I walk toward him, watching me without saying another word until I'm in front of him, and crouch down between his parted legs. I could say I don't know why I did it, but I do. The pain on his face is as deep as the pain in my heart, and for both of us, I just want it to stop. I only wish I knew how to make it.

Placing a hand on each of his thighs, I lower my head face down until my forehead is resting against the seat, and say loud enough I'm sure he can hear me, "I never meant to hurt you."

"I know," he says after a beat, his hands threading their way through my hair at the same time. "You wouldn't be this close if I thought you had."

I hate how the tears come then, and I vocalize the way it makes me feel to him because I hope he can make it stop. "I've never felt so much in my life. My emotions have always been...steady. I hurt so badly, and now that I've let myself cry, I can't seem to stop. Even when it isn't coming out of my eyes in the form of tears, I still feel like my heart is weeping all the time."

He moves his hands from simply resting in my hair to stroking it, and this little comfort is all it takes for me to fall into my pain, knowing he'll catch me. Trusting he will.

"I want it to stop," I choke out through a sob. "Make it stop."

I don't know how he does it, maybe because I'm so caught up in my grief I don't notice, but he hauls me into his lap, and cradles my body against his. Tucking my head into the crook of his neck, he rests his chin on top of my head as one arm holds me tight around my waist, the other continuing to stroke my hair while I begin to bawl like a baby.

"I can't," he replies to my brokenhearted demand. "I wish I could, but I can't. I'll hold you however long you need though, sweetheart."

And he does. I don't know how long he sits there cradling me in his arms as I cry into his shoulder, but when my sobs turn into hiccups he hands me a tissue. Wiping my eyes and blowing my nose, he lets me go with marked reluctance as I lift my head, and then climb off his lap to throw the tissue away in the trash next to the desk.

Taking a deep breath and letting it out slowly, I lean on the desk, crossing my arms over my chest as he stares at me with hooded eyes.

My voice is scratchy as I ask, "Where do we go from here?"

"I don't know," he says, lifting his hand in a

helpless gesture, and frowns. "It's up to you, Caroline. I think we both know what I want."

"Me."

"Yeah, you." He brings his chair forward until I'm trapped between him and the desk. Sliding his hands up each of my bare legs, his hands slide around the back and under my skirt until he grips my ass in his hands. "No matter how angry or hurt I was, that hasn't changed. I want you in every way, Caroline."

I do my best to ignore the small flame of desire bursting to life at his touch, feeling as if I don't deserve it, and it isn't right to feel like this right now. Slamming my eyes shut, as if not seeing him will make it go away, I say, "Even with me being shattered like this?"

"You're not shattered, not by far. You've been hit hard enough to disorient you, make your ears ring, and your world seem like it doesn't make sense. You might even have a figurative concussion. But you're not broken, sweetheart. Your world will right itself, as long as you accept it's forever changed, and there's nothing you can do about it otherwise."

As my skirt slightly rises, my eyes pop open, and as I look down, I find him looking up at me, his eyes flaming with the desire that aches to spread through me if I'd let it. One which he tries to ignite by moving his focus from my face to between my legs, helping himself along by lifting me a little until the desk supports me enough he can spread them, lifting them over his shoulders. His actions leave me scrambling for something to hold onto, to anchor me as I teeter on the edge of more than just the desk, and the closest thing to grab is his hair, so that's where my hands end up.

"Ben—"

"Shh. Don't talk." His breath is hot as it brushes against my labia, which he's exposed by using one finger the fabric covering me to the side. "If you're going to cry, I want it to be with pleasure, not pain."

My legs tremble, a small moan breaking through as he spreads me open with his fingers, and uses his tongue to tease me. My hands tighten in his hair as he licks up, circles the tip of his tongue around my clit once, twice, before taking his tongue back down.

"God, you're so fucking wet," he says after removing his mouth, only to start all over again.

And I do weep, so conflicted inside, as I'm not sure how to reconcile my grief over Nathan with the need for closeness with Benedict.

A big part of me wants to stop him, but another part doesn't. Then, for the first time in so fucking long, I'm not thinking about Nathan, or my pain, or anything else except Benedict and the pleasure he's giving me. The ache in my heart is muted for a few moments by the burning one between my legs, and all I can get out as my body spirals toward orgasm is, "please."

I don't know what I'm asking for, but he does.

He lifts me up and away from the desk, and I've only seconds to register him pulling his mouth away before my back is flat against the floor, his body covering mine at the same time he crushes my lips beneath his. With one of my legs wrapped around his waist, a heartbeat or two passes before he finds and thrusts into me, meeting only a little resistance before he's as deep as he can go. Grasping my hip painfully, he pulls out and slams back in, and both of us moan at how absolutely fucking great the other feels.

Keeping our mouths locked together, he moves again and this time, he doesn't stop.

I never understood until this exact moment how someone could fuck me so hard and so fast, making me feel as if I'm nothing more than a sex object, but also make me feel surrounded, and loved, and briefly, whole. He's making me feel that way as he thrusts into me so hard, repeatedly, enough it hurts, but his kisses are oddly paced so much slower. The way our mouths meld makes it clear he's loving me, trying to please me, and sharing how deeply my unintentional rejection tore him apart while still trying to make me come fast and strong.

But then he pauses, leaning up as I let him go with my arms and my mouth reluctantly, only to grin down at me as he shrugs out of his coat which he tosses to the side. His face is shiny from his exertion, and I deliberately rotate my hips, causing him to groan and slam his eyes shut while loosening his tie.

I'm impatient though, and when I grab the end of the tie and tug, his eyes open to meet mine as he lifts a brow in question.

"I like when you fuck me in your suit. Don't undress anymore."

"I'm hot."

"Yeah. You are."

He continues to stare down at me, not moving even as I hold his tie, our bodies still connected in the most intimate way. I don't like what goes on with his eyes though, which eventually leads to his whole face going serious, and he pulls out.

"I don't want to do this here." Standing above me, he holds out a hand to help me up if I want it. "Come spend the night with me."

Lying as I am on the floor, in the position he left me in, my mouth drops open in disbelief. "You're seriusly going to leave me hanging? What—"

"I haven't slept," he states, leaning down to lift

me and place me on my feet, his eyes piercing mine with his need. "Have you?"

He's not asking about last night, or even the night before, but all the time we were apart. And he already knows the answer.

I say it anyway. "No."

Bending down, he presses a kiss to my stomach before covering it with my shirt, and lowering my skirt back into place. Then, slipping his hand into mine, he interlaces our fingers together and smiles.

"Come home with me. Please."

I say the only thing I can say. The only thing left to say at all because it's what we both want. What we both need.

"Okay."

And for the first time since Nathan died, the vise which has been squeezing my heart loosens a little, letting me finally feel the truth about how I'm not as alone as I thought I was.

CHAPTER TWENTY-EIGHT

When I first wake up the next morning, I'm disoriented.

Like many mornings since we first met, me and Benedict are snuggling, his left leg thrown over mine and his arm about my waist to keep me from escaping his grasp. I recognize his room instantly, though, and I quickly remember how I ended up here in his bed with him.

His breathing is deep and steady. I feel it against my neck, each puff of air causing the area it touches to tingle, and has me wishing he would wake up to make good on the promise his body is making to mine. Especially since after we'd climbed into bed without any clothes on, it wasn't long before we passed out, so we never got to finish what he started in his office.

But it was after his statement last night, about not having slept, that I looked past my own grief to see how tired he truly was. How tired he looked, with an exhaustion that went deeper than on the surface. So there's no way I'm even attempting to move right now, or wake him.

Only problem is lying here wide awake with time to think inevitably leads to my thoughts to focus on Nathan.

It's impossible to think of him as any other name than Nathan. It's the name I knew him and loved him by, and the name I'll never forget as long as I live. And while he'll always live on in my thoughts, I can't help but wish I had something of his to keep with me. It'll never happen now, as all his property was sold off to pay debts I didn't know he had, and that included the house we lived in.

We weren't married, so I had no rights, and although my parents had made sure all my stuff was removed from the property, everything else was long gone by now. Except a box with a letter addressed to me attached to it, which the cops had found in a drawer in the bedroom where he was shot, and they'd given to me at some point. I don't really know when, as most of the memories surrounding my life then are hazy due to my shock and disbelief.

A box I've known contains a ring he intended

to propose to me with, but the letter still sits, unopened. I've kept it in my stuff, knowing one day I'll get up the courage to read what I know is probably a goodbye letter. However, it won't be the words of a dying man, but the words of the man I love telling me he's leaving me. And even though everything went terribly wrong, I'm not sure I can handle reading him telling me goodbye. Because even with all that happened, all these months later I'm still able to feel his arms around me those last moments we spent together in the club, and him telling me he loves me and will see me in the morning.

I don't wish to replace the last moments of my life with him for harsh reality.

Benedict shifts behind me, his arms tightening as if in reflex, and after pressing a gentle kiss on my bare shoulder, whispers, "Morning. Where were you? Looked like you were lost in thought."

"I was, but I'm not now. I was letting you rest."

"Caroline, turn over."

With a soft laugh, I say, "I would but you're kinda pinning me down in case you didn't notice."

"Oh, right." He releases me with a chuckle of his own. "Been so long—"

"Shh." I cut him off with a hand over his mouth as I finish turning over. "I get it."

He licks my palm, breaking into a full out laugh

as I yank it away with a mock look of disgust, before hauling me back into his arms.

"Much better. I like when I can see your face. Tells me everything I need to know." His eyes drop to my neck, his voice thick with emotion when he finally speaks. "When did you take it off?"

I reach up to my bare neck, specifically to where the charm used to hang on the necklace he'd given me, the action something I haven't done in a while now except for when I opened his emails, and smile at him sadly when he returns his gaze to mine. "About a week after leaving, I—I was so upset, especially because my parents were suffocating me, and I just lost it. I had a total meltdown, where I started hitting and throwing things, to the point my father had to physically restrain me when he came to see what the hell was going on. I didn't remember most of it, but they had to have me sedated, and when I woke up, it was gone. I had scratches all over me, even on my neck, and my father told me it probably got snagged on something and broke, perhaps even when I fought him as he tried to hold me. We don't know what happened to it and I never was able to find it."

Moving my hand from my neck to his chest, I slide it up and around until it rests on the back of his neck and whisper, "I already felt so empty, when I woke up and it was gone, it just made me feel so much worse. Because I couldn't replace it. I couldn't fix anything, it made me feel so fucking helpless—"

"Shh, it's okay." He cuts me off by placing one finger over my lips. "All I care about is you, Caroline. You, like that necklace, are one-hundred percent unique. And irreplaceable."

"What?"

With a sheepish grin, he shrugs, but his eyes continue to stare into mine, burning bright with everything he feels. "You couldn't get a necklace with that charm anywhere if you tried. I had it made for you." My lower lip wobbles at this, and he growls while bringing his face close to mine. "No, don't cry. Don't you dare fucking cry about it, because I don't give a shit about that necklace. You, and only you, is all I cared about the whole time you were gone."

"But—"

"No." Pressing his lips against mine, he rolls me onto my back and brings his body above mine, moving to put my arms above my head as I try to wrap them around his neck. Holding them there by the wrists, he deepens the kiss, for so long that when he finally stops, I'm breathing so hard I can't speak.

He, however, doesn't seem to have that problem, as he says inches from my mouth, "I didn't come after you this time, because I knew it wasn't about me. You know how fucking difficult it was for me not to hop on a plane and follow you, make you talk to me, let me hold you like I wanted to? I've never, in my whole goddamned life, wanted to do anything more than I wanted to do that. But I didn't. Even though the last fucking look I saw on your face was so heartbroken and filled with disbelief, and I wanted to protect you from ever feeling like that ever again."

"That's why you emailed me every day?"

"Yeah, even after I realized you weren't reading them, because you told Ethan about how you weren't even checking your email at one point. I think it was about two months after you left."

With a gasp, I whisper, "I don't understand. Why keep going after you knew?"

"Because." He grips my wrists tighter as he rocks our lower bodies together, letting out a naughty chuckle when I moan. "Even if you weren't reading them, I wanted you to know I didn't forget about you at all. I made sure to send something every day, even if it was just to tell you I love you. Pretty sure there's a fuck ton of those."

Straight up pure guilt and a little bit of anger at

myself course through me at his admission. "Oh, Benedict… I—I'm such a bitch. I'm sorry."

"Nah, you're not. If you were truly a bitch, I wouldn't want to fuck you as much as I do right now. Unlike many of the men I'm acquainted with, my heart is connected to my cock, and both are extremely happy right now."

"My heart is, too," I admit softly, accompanying my words with a frown. "And it feels so nice, but also so wrong, all at the same time."

"That's okay. You may not be all right for a long time, but as long as you don't shut me out and push me away, I'm not going anywhere."

I believe he means it, and while I know I've personally got a long way to go, I know my relationship with him is on its way to finding its rhythm once more. I know I'm bound to fuck up, even though I hope I don't, but for now, I let it all go to enjoy this time with him before life intrudes as it always does.

Relaxing underneath him completely, I tell him what he needs to hear, something I haven't said in a long time and will say so much more now because of how precious time really is. "I love you."

That's all it takes. That's all he needs and all I need, and his lips devour mine as he uses his free hand to lift one of my legs around his waist. Then, between our bodies, he guides himself into place, pushing just the tip in as he mutters against my mouth, "I love you, too. And we're gonna go real slow, because I wanna enjoy every fucking minute of this. Of you."

He lets go of my wrists, smiling as I lift them and wrap them around his neck once more, and captures my lips once again. Gripping my hip once more, he makes love to my mouth while moving against me, each small thrust sinking him deeper and deeper into my pussy. His mouth and tongue swallow every sound of pleasure I make, and soon his gentle strokes take him to the tip and back until he can go no further, the pace keeping the fire going, but not making it rise. And while I love this rather gentle love making, I can't handle it right now, because I'm not used to it from *him*. It's usually fast and rough when I'm with him, and right now, I need things with him to be familiar. Less lovemaking like.

I pull my lips away to beg, "Please. Go faster, I... I can't handle this..."

He pauses in his strokes, looks me square in the eyes, and whatever he sees makes him nod. Pulling out, he says with a chuckle, "Turn over and on your knees."

I see him grab a pillow as I do as he said, and I

let out an audible sigh of relief, which turns into a gasp as his hand smacks my ass. Then, he sticks the pillow under me to elevate my ass into the air, but presses his hand on my back until I'm resting comfortably.

"Now," he says while spreading my legs a little until I feel him settle between them. "Extend your arms and lock those naughty little fingers of yours on the headboard and don't say another word."

I do, breaking his rules almost instantly to whisper with a little excitement, "Are we going to play a game?"

"Hey." He lands a semi-hard slap on my ass and I jump, yet manage to prevent myself from yelping. "I said don't say anything." When I remain silent, he soothes the spot he smacked and says, "Yes, we're going to play a game. My favorite. I'm sure you remember it quite well."

I do, and it's exactly what I want right now. I'm so glad he gets it.

But, instead of picking up where we left off, he leans his body over mine, and runs his palm from the top of my head down until he reaches my bare back. "How kinky are you, Caroline? Do you even know?" He laughs when I stay quiet and says, "You can answer my questions."

"No." My face heats as I admit, "I just did

whatever... you know, whatever you or..." His name sticks in my throat so I just skip it because we both know who. "I don't think I've done anything too out there... I guess?"

"Interesting."

I can practically feel the wheels in his head turning, and I know if I looked back, he'll have his head tilted just a little as he contemplates what I've said. I want to ask why it's interesting, but he said I could answer his questions, and I know that means *only* his questions.

"You're probably wondering why that's interesting." He leans away from me back to his original position, running his hand down my spine as he does so, and then cups one of my ass cheeks at the end. "And it's interesting because you exhibit a lot of tendencies that pretty much indicate you're a submissive."

Stiffening, I give him a vehement shake of my head, because I may not know much, but I know about that. And I'm not that.

"I'm not."

Whoops.

"Yes, I'm betting you are. And I'll let that little slip pass because by the way you just reacted, you've taken that as an insult for some reason." Using both of his hands, he runs them up and down the side of my thighs as if to soothe me, and says in a gentle tone, "It's not an insult. As a matter of fact, I'm quite pleased. Want to know why?"

"No."

"Too bad." He chuckles as I sigh because I figured he would tell me anyway. "I bet you've got the idea in your head that a submissive is a doormat. Someone who lets everyone walk all over her, control her, use her. Am I far off?"

"No."

"I thought so. What threw me is the first time we were alone, that night in my club in my office, you kissed me first. After that, I've pretty much always made the first move, but I never thought about it much. You like someone else to take the lead when it comes to sex. That's undeniable, isn't it?"

I stay quiet, taking in what he's saying and tossing it around my head, trying to think about all the times we've had sex and who started it. And realize, yep, he did for the most part. Dammit.

"You're a strong woman, Caroline. You truly are. You're smart, funny, kind, and definitely not a doormat. You may not know what you want to do with your life, but you certainly don't let anyone else tell you what to do with it. You might need a little nudge every now and then to acknowledge what everybody else already knows, but who doesn't? You know how to give love unconditionally more than how to receive it, but we'll work on that."

He stops his stroking and leans back over my body, one hand going to my hair to stroke it, yet stops halfway down. "You're a natural submissive, Caroline, and the proof is in the fact you give into me every time, aim to please me every time we're together without even hesitating. Do you think what we do together makes you a doormat?"

"N-no. Not at all."

"And why would you? We both enjoy each other immensely and now I realize it's because we complement one another in that way along with the many other ways we already do. As for why I'm pleased, well, isn't that obvious? I have you."

For some reason, I feel like sobbing all of a sudden, and strangely he must recognize it, because he moves his hand from my hair down to around my body and hugs me as he presses soft kisses on my shoulder. After a few moments, he presses one final long kiss and pulls away, getting back into position as he says, "I think that's enough talking for now. You ready?"

Relaxing my body, I give him a simple hum of approval.

When his cock enters me, he does it so

agonizingly slow it makes me want to growl with frustration because I want him to go fast, and move my hips back toward him to try and get what I want.

He pulls out and smacks each of my cheeks once which turns me on and makes me laugh all at once.

"Now you're just being a brat on purpose," he says, but his amusement is clear. "Don't try to top from the bottom. You know I'll give you what you want."

I don't know what he means, but right now, I don't care anyway as I break the rules to tell him, "Well, give me what I want then, because I'm hungry and I want to eat."

"I'm trying to feed you!"

"Food, Benedict! Food!"

He thrust into me hard then, gripping my hips tight to maintain control as he gives me what I want, to the point my fingers turn white from clenching the posts in the headboard as much as I can. But unlike the first time we did this, I can't stay silent. I enjoy this, I enjoy him too much, and every thrust into me makes me cry out with enjoyment. And he doesn't seem to care because when my body grows more taut the closer to coming I get, he lets go of one of my hips to slide his hand between my legs and touch me just like I need him to.

When I shatter around him at his touch, he follows closely behind, bringing our bodies close together as he groans into my neck. And once he moves, he collapses on the bed beside me, and I crawl into his arms where I want to be more than anything else right now.

CHAPTER TWENTY-NINE

My actual internship — and that of my two classmates, Ingrid and Lee — at *Club Play* actually starts immediately. So, instead of going to class, we go to work, and turn in our papers and assignments online. I worried about Benedict and I being together, and him technically being my boss for the semester, but last night at dinner he told me not to, that he'd taken care of it.

I find out how today when we are taken into his office once we arrive and another man joins us. I've never seen him before, but aesthetically, he's an attractive man around the same age as Benedict if I had to guess, and one who exhibits the power he knows he has. A little taller than Benedict, he's got blond hair and light blue eyes, and when he catches me studying him, he simply gives me a smirk and looks away. When Benedict clears his throat, I can't help the guilty flush that comes over me as I rip my gaze away and focus on him, but he grins at me as if he's quite aware of the visual appeal of his friend.

"Ingrid. Lee. Caroline." He nods at each of us individually as he extends an arm toward the man. "I'd like you to meet Felix Stratford. As you are aware, I own three clubs, but I only manage this one on a day-to-day basis, even though I'm involved in all of them on every level. Felix manages the second *Club Play*, which is located about an hour away, and will be mentoring this semester as well."

He flicks his gaze toward me for a moment, but then focuses on Ingrid and Lee, who are sitting in the chairs in front of his desk while I stand. "I don't know if you two are aware, but I'm in a relationship with Caroline, and your teacher assigned your placements without knowing about it. I informed him of this fact, which is why you two will be working with me, and Caroline will be working with Felix to keep everything aboveboard. Moving people around would've caused too many issues for your teacher since his placements were based on your records and what skills he thought you needed to work on the most, which is why you were assigned to me. Any problem with this?"

They both shrug and then shake their heads. If they are anything like me, they don't care, they just want to get this semester over with so they can graduate like I do. And I'm not at all disappointed that we won't work together, since I mostly think about sex with Benedict when I'm around him, and I wouldn't learn a thing because of it. Although I do feel bad I thought he picked me on purpose before he knew how things would go down between us, something we already had a good laugh about.

"Good. Now as to what we will cover..."

I end up taking a seat on the couch as he goes on and on about pretty much all things I already know about the club, so I feel free to check out of listening. Not that I'm obvious about it. I keep my eyes on him, but in my head, I'm thinking about another conversation we had while lying in bed last night, about to go to sleep.

He said he knew I probably hadn't thought about it, but considering my relationship with Nathan, did I also consider our relationship to be open as well? I told him I didn't know, and when I asked him why he wanted to know, he told me that since things had changed, we would have to define our relationship. New rules and all.

I hadn't said anything after that other than I'd have to think on it and he seemed okay with letting it go for now.

And now, here I am thinking about it, and the truth is, I don't know the answer to his question. Even though our relationship started off with me being in one with Nathan, and him being with Miranda, now that we weren't any longer, although neither of by choice, what did that mean for us? I know he's right; we will have to define where we both stand, and what we want.

Problem is, I have no idea, made harder by the fact I never wanted to be in this position. Certainly never thought I would be, either. I probably should've asked him what he wants, but I'm fairly sure I know already anyway.

He wants me, and only me, but just like with Miranda, he'll do what I want because he'll want to make me happy. I won't do to him what Miranda did though. If I decide I want us to have an open relationship, and it's not what he wants, then I'll have a tough decision to make.

I can't prevent a little smile on my face as I wonder if this is how Nathan felt when he wanted to date me, and was worried I'd turn him down because of it, or when he approached Rissa. I never asked him if he still would've dated me if I had told him no, I couldn't deal with the fact he wanted to be with someone else other than me forever. A question I'll never get the answer to now.

And then I refocus on Benedict speaking at the front of the room, realizing while he did deal with the fact Miranda wanted to open their relationship, he hadn't truly been happy about it. It had been a last ditch effort to keep their relationship from falling apart completely, and it hadn't worked, because their relationship wasn't solid before they opened it up, especially since she'd been sleeping with Len long before she asked for permission.

When the couch cushion dips next to me, I whip my head to find Felix sitting down next to me with a smile.

"You appear terribly bored," he says in a low voice as he leans toward me in a conspiratorial manner. "I sure hope you won't have that same look on your face every time we're working together this semester." When I just raise a brow at him, his smile widens. "I've never been involved in helping Ben with an internship before; he brought me in just for you."

"Did he?" I keep my voice low so we don't disturb anyone else. "Well, you should count yourself lucky then, as I'm an A-plus student."

"So you're an overachiever and I should worry about you telling me how to do my job instead?"

"Probably."

"Excellent. Then you'll be able to take over and I can go on my very overdue vacation."

"Sounds like a plan," I say, unable to keep my lips from curving up in amusement, especially at the fact he seems to take my joking in stride. "Where would you go?"

His answer is instantaneous. "England."

"Oh. I just came back from there."

"I know. Ben told me."

"Oh." I look down into my lap, focusing on my fingers as they fidget with my phone. "I suppose he told you everything."

"Yes. It's only fair, don't you think, since we'll be working together? I need to understand your state of mind, especially if there are days you might not make it to class."

His assumption annoys me. "I've never missed a day in anything I've ever done."

Covering my hands with his, and causing them to still in their movements, I glance up at him to find his eyes filled with what looks like sympathy. Or pity. Either way, I don't want either, and I scowl at him.

He takes his hand off with a sigh, but his gaze doesn't leave mine. "I'm not saying you will, but losing a loved one is hard. It's possible you might have a bad day, and so, I'm telling you I will understand if you can't make it at some point. Just call and let me know, at the very least, all right?"

"Of course."

"Good. He's finishing now, then we will go and you will start your first day."

We both turn our attention back to Benedict who is saying, "And finally. Your class is three credits. You each need one-hundred and thirty-five hours. Spread over fifteen weeks, because your last week are finals and you need to focus on studying, you will do nine hours a week." He nods at Ingrid and Lee. "We will go over your schedules today and make them so you will each work with me individually." Then, he looks at me. "Caroline, your schedule is up to you and Felix. Any questions?"

"Nope," I say while standing. "I'm all set, then?"

"Yes, you are free to go." He doesn't linger on me, dismissing me in words and action as he walks behind his desk, and sits down. "Now, you two..."

"I need to get some lunch," Felix says as we walk out the door and shut it behind us. "Would you like to join me, or do you just want to meet me at the club in say, an hour and a half?"

"Thanks for the offer, but I'll meet you there."

He nods and walks off, and after a trip to the ladies room, I stop at the bar to chat with Frank. Who, of course, comes around and envelops me in a tight bear hug.

"You forgot to give me one the other night," he murmurs into my hair before releasing me. "But I forgive you because you only had eyes for one person as you walked out."

"Thanks. I was real afraid you'd spit in my drink because I forgot."

He laughs at my obvious joke, shaking his head as he steps back behind the bar, which is pretty slow at the moment. "Jokes aside, darlin', how are you really doing?" As I take a seat with a sigh, he makes me a glass of soda and sets it in front of me. "That bad, huh?"

"I'm not really sure it'll ever get easier."

"Has to be better than nearly nine months ago; you're sitting back here talking to me, right?"

"You might be right."

"When am I ever wrong?" He looks to the left, then to the right, and then back at me with a wink as he leans in to whisper, "I tell you what though, Miranda's baby is adorable, and I didn't think that would be the case."

I almost choke on the soda in my mouth, but manage to avoid it, swallowing it down before giving Frank an 'I can't believe you just said that' look. And okay, I did have to hold back a laugh. "Well, they are both attractive people, but even good looking people can have some not-so-good-looking babies, so you might've been right. Just... just don't ever say that out loud again. It's not socially acceptable."

"Darlin', I'm not stupid. But I knew I could trust you."

"Yeah. And I bet you were a cute baby, weren't you?"

"Uh, have you looked at me?" He points a finger at his own face. "I'm fugly and always have been."

"Oh, shut up. You are not." I down my soda after glancing at my watch, and then stand up while teasing him. "See you later, Frankenstein. It's time for me to get to work."

He chuckles and lifts a hand in response. "Later."

Once I'm in my car and on my way, I'm about halfway there when I realize I'm humming along to the songs playing on the radio for the first time since Nathan's death.

The first four weeks of school, and my internship, fly by with no drama or anything.

In a lot of ways, even with the way everything's clearly changed, many things seem to have stayed the same.

Once Benedict and I got our feelings out in the open, we basically returned to our rhythm we had before. I spend a lot of my time with him, even though I've kept my room at Ethan's, but it's almost unnecessary. A fact I think Ethan's grateful for; not because he doesn't love me, but because he enjoys the fact he gets a lot of alone time with Destiny. And me? I don't want to make any decisions I might regret because I want to be really sure before making any. At this point, I'm not sure of anything except that I'm tired of not being sure, of course.

I still want the pain to go away. I love Nathan

so much, he's always on my mind, even when I don't want him to be, because it often makes me want to breakdown when I really can't.

I also know I'm healing, although most of the time it doesn't feel like it. But every day it gets easier to breathe, to admit I'll never see him again in my head and not feel as if my heart is bleeding, and it means I'm seeing my life for what it really is.

Blessed.

When I came back, I hadn't wanted to, because I knew my whole life would be right in my face. Every choice I made before, everyone who knew me and Nathan, and every single place we'd ever gone together...they were inescapable. It hurt to drive by where we used to live and the first time I did it, I had to pull to the side of the road after anxiety got the best of me.

But coming back...I believed it saved me. I feel love from every direction. From Ethan, from Frank, and most especially, from Benedict. With every action, every word, he's there for me even if he doesn't understand. If he sees a tear start to slide down my cheek, even in the most random of moments where he can't make a connection as to why I'm starting to cry, he will just hug me until I let him know it's okay to let go.

We still haven't defined our relationship, but Benedict hasn't asked again, and I'm grateful for that. He knows we will talk about it when I've made sense of all the changes in my life. Until then, he simply said we should take it day-by-day and have fun.

So, I'm taking that advice.

And tonight, I'm going to do something I haven't since I came back, because it's one more thing I need to do. It's also another step in healing.

I'm spending the evening at the club with my friends and having fun, just like I used to with Nathan.

"You ready, Caro?"

Closing the lid to my laptop, I slide off the bed and put on my shoes, and then smile at him as I grab my purse. "Yep. Let's go."

It's not long until we arrive, and after getting inside, Ethan and Destiny immediately go off to dance while I walk to Benedict's office. As always, I don't bother knocking, and when I open the door, I find him standing behind his desk shrugging into his suit jacket.

When he lifts his head and catches sight of me, he freezes, his gaze burning bright as he takes in my outfit. Starting at my hair which is curled and falling around my shoulders, down to my soft white blouse, hip-hugging blue jeans, and black ankle boots.

"Yes," I say with a grin when his disbelieving eyes return to mine. "I'm wearing jeans. Shocked?"

His smile matches mine as he stalks toward me. "A little, but god, you're gorgeous in anything. I can't even compete."

"Shut up. You'd be hot even if you wore a trash bag."

"They look tight," he comments, chuckling as he stops in front of me. "I'm not even sure I'd be able to stick my hand down your pants."

"They are. But they're real comfortable. They better be for what I paid for them."

"Good jeans are worth every cent."

"Oh?" I lift a brow at him as he wraps his arms around me and pulls me close to his body. "I've never seen you wear a pair of jeans."

"I do own several pairs but it's just easier to be dressed and ready to work at all times. Maybe I'll give you a private showing, though, if you ask nicely."

"You will wear a pair if I have to hold you down and put them on you myself. How's that for nicely?"

He slides his hands down my ass and squeezes my cheeks, making me squeal, and then we both jump at the sound of Ethan's voice.

"Hey, lovebirds." Ethan grins as we both turn toward him, Benedict with a smirk on his face, and mine all flushed. "How 'bout making it out here to join us sometime today?"

"Yeah, yeah," I grumble as Benedict lets me go, slipping his hand into mine. "We're coming now. Shoo."

Ethan turns away, walking off with a laugh.

Once Benedict locks his office, we head toward the bar. Squeezing our way past people, we finally reach it and at only finding one available stool, he says, "You take it. I'm more than happy to stand beside you."

"You just wanna be able to cop a feel without anybody seeing. Don't lie."

He winks at me as I laugh, and steps real close, resting one of his hands on my back while the other is on the bar counter. Leaning in, he skims his nose from my ear down to where my neck meets my shoulder, kisses me softly, and after taking a deep breath says, "You smell so fucking delicious. Like chocolate. How'd you manage that? Did you bake some chocolate chip muffins and then roll around in them?"

With a laugh, I shake my head. "No, that would be wasteful. It's simply chocolate perfume."

"Oh." He sounds disappointed and I laugh when he says, "I won't lick you then since I'm sure it won't taste as yummy as it smells."

"Yeah, it's not like flavored chapstick."

He feathers kisses up my neck, then along my jaw, until he reaches my lips where he pauses to say, "You don't need anything on your lips to make me want to taste them. They're enticing enough on their own."

It's like we're in our own world when he puts his lips on mine, his teeth grabbing my bottom lip for a second before letting go, and giving the spot his teeth had nipped a lick as he chuckles. People talking, the music, everything...it just fades when I'm with him, and it's nice. Okay, it's more than nice; it practically makes my heart sing.

"You're so fucking lucky you wore those jeans, Caroline." The hand on my back slides down until he can run his finger along the bare skin above the rim of my jeans, then down to a cheek, where it rests against where my ass meets the seat and he can't go any further. "Because if you weren't, I'm not sure I'd be able to keep myself from spreading those legs of yours—"

A loud cough real close makes us both jump and look over to the left only to find Rissa standing there, her face flushed scarlet. I'm sure it matches mine, and Benedict gets completely out of my space as I stare at her in shock. I haven't seen her since school let out, not even when Nathan died, and I'm not sure why she's here now.

"Rissa—"

"I know," she says, clearing her throat as her hands fidget with her clutch. "One of my friends called me while I was on break and I just couldn't make myself come back here, not for anything. Especially since he broke up with me before he left for his trip."

This is news to me, and I'm sure my face is filled with confusion. "What?"

"I don't know." She shrugs and gives me a weak smile. "He said it wasn't me, and I believed him, because him — and you — were always so open with me, even though I was still hurt. And once I find out everything about... about..." She slams her eyes shut, clearing her throat, no doubt to shove her voice past the tears clogging her throat; a feeling I'm all too familiar with. "Well, even then I couldn't be mad because he helped me so much with some issues I've had. His love and understanding..."

"I'm glad for you," I say when her voice trails off and her eyes fill with tears. "And I'm glad he helped you. I don't know why he broke up with you before he left, but he made you as happy as he made me, and that's all that matters."

"I know." She swallows, her smile wobbly even as genuine happiness shines in her eyes, and gives a small nod toward her left shoulder. "My boyfriend is over here. We started dating six months ago. He's terrific. I... I felt guilty at first, like I shouldn't date so soon after... but then I remember what both you and Nathan told me when you sat me down that one day."

I remember too. When she holds out her hand toward me, I take it, and she squeezes it, saying softly, "You two said the heart didn't have any earthly boundaries. That even when it hurt, even when you thought you couldn't care anymore than you already do, or have any more love, it expands so you can fit everything you want and need right inside of it. And I knew Nathan would understand. He'd be happy for me; two months or ten or a year or two, he'd just be happy I decided to let love in even if I thought I couldn't do it again."

With another press of my hand, she moves her gaze from my face to Benedict's, and back again. "I'm so happy for both of you. I just wanted to tell you that." Dropping my hand, she steps back with a nod toward where she last indicated her boyfriend was. "I should get going. Pete's waiting on me."

As she turns to go, I stand up and say, "Wait."

She faces me again with a raised brow, and after rubbing my hands together nervously, I step toward her until I'm close enough to do the one thing I've never done with her. It also happens to be the one thing I hardly ever do with anyone of my own volition.

consider leaving a rating & review. I would appreciate it a lot!*

Join my reader's list to stay up-to-date on new releases, giveaways, events & more by visiting my website (authorviolethaze.com).
No spam ever!

ABOUT THE AUTHOR

Violet Haze is a big fan of writing and reading romance. The autistic mother of one, she currently spends her days writing, reading, procrastinating, playing violin and learning guitar, & listening to her son play video games she doesn't understand.

For information on other books you can read, including links to ALL the vendors, visit her website:
www.authorviolethaze.com!

Want to contact Violet?
Email her at: violet@authorviolethaze.com
Locate her by searching "Author Violet Haze" on Instagram, Facebook, and Twitter!